What's in your Garden?
A book for young explorers

Colin Spedding

Brambleby Books Ltd.

What's in your Garden? A book for young explorers
© Colin Spedding 2010

All Rights Reserved

No part of this book may be reproduced in any form by photocopying or by any electronic or mechanical means, including information, storage or retrieval systems, without permission in writing from both the copyright owner and the publisher of this book.

ISBN-13: 978 0 9553928

Published 2010 by
BRAMBLEBY BOOKS
Luton, Bedfordshire, UK
www.bramblebybooks.co.uk

Cover design and book layout by Creatix Design Services
Painting on cover by the artist Isla Woiwod

Printed on FSC paper by
Cambrian Printers, Aberystwyth, UK.

What's in your Garden?

ACKNOWLEDGEMENTS

The whole book was read for me by Michaela Macphie, then aged 8, chapter by chapter, as they were written. This was organised by my daughter, Mrs Lucy Weston, who then told me Michaela's reactions – whether the words were too big, whether the drawings were useful, and so on. I then rewrote each chapter and this was read again until we got it right!

I am greatly indebted for all this help, as I am to my secretary, Mrs Mary Jones, who performed much the same task, as well as typing the result.

DEDICATION

Michaela Macphie
Emma Macphie
Lucy Weston

Contents

- 12 About the Author
- 13 Preface
- 14 What's in your Garden?
- 22 Butterflies and Moths
- 26 Bees, Wasps and Ants
- 32 Nests
- 40 Eggs
- 45 Hedges, Trees and Bushes
- 50 Seeds
- 56 What's under Logs and Stones?
- 59 What's in the long Grass?
- 64 The Hunters
- 70 The Hunted
- 74 What's in the Pond?
- 79 The Garden at Night
- 84 Glossary

What's in your Garden?

ABOUT THE AUTHOR

Professor Sir Colin Spedding has dedicated his long career to the study of biology, especially including animal welfare. He has a passionate interest in how living things interrelate and how such ecologies are shaped by the organism's form, function, reproduction and behaviour. He is also very dedicated to the education of young people, having worked with primary school children for over 17 years, showing them the organisation and complexity of the living world, including its beauty. Professor Spedding explains the natural world around us from the perspective of a garden using clear line drawings, complemented with colour photographs. He aims to show how the apparently familiar is more fascinating than may be imagined. This is a truly inspiring approach, one that will surely encourage young people to see the world through 'new' eyes.

PREFACE

I wrote this book because I found that a previous book, *The Natural History of a Garden*, was being used by parents and grandparents to show children what was in their gardens. So I thought, "Why not write a book that children could read for themselves?" and this is it.

It is written for children of 7 to 11 years of age and the illustrations are also drawn for this age group. However, I have found that people of all ages appreciate a book that is clear and free from jargon or as Einstein put, "as simple as possible – but no simpler."

What's in your Garden?

Many people think gardens are just about plants.

What do you think?

I expect you see lots of animals as well.

Think of a nice sunny summer's day and what do you see?

Flowers?
Butterflies?
Birds? … What else?

Snails, spiders, earwigs, ladybirds?

All these will be found in most gardens and all gardens are home to some animals.

Of course, it depends how big your garden is, where it is (in the town or the country) and what sort of a garden it is (full of trees, bushes or with a big lawn, for example).

Do you have a fish pond? Are there any fish in it?

Or a vegetable garden? What does that grow? Cabbages, Brussels sprouts, lettuces, radishes?

All these are grown so that we can eat them, but other things eat them as well, like caterpillars of the Large White butterfly.

Does your vegetable garden have any flowers?

Do the vegetables produce flowers?

If we let them grow beyond the time when we would usually pick them, they do grow flowers: but these are not very big, colourful or nice to look at. Why is this?

Over many years, we have chosen plants either to grow big leaves or roots that we can eat (these are the vegetables) or to grow big, colourful flowers for the main garden (as decoration).

So, here are some more interesting questions:

Why do plants have flowers?

You will notice that they attract insects, such as butterflies and bees – but what other insects do you see on flowers?

Flowers need these insects to carry their pollen to other flowers, which helps them to make their seeds. I expect you've noticed that nearly all flowers, if they are not picked, slowly wither away and, in their place, seed heads appear. These are of many different shapes and each contains lots of seeds, some of them very small.

Seeds can be easily seen in bluebells. When the blue, bell-shaped flowers are gone, they leave behind papery cups full of small, shiny, dark-brown seeds. You can plant these wherever you want more bluebells to grow. So the plant has the flowers to attract insects which again help it to make seeds.

The insects don't just visit the flowers because they look nice. They are attracted to the flowers because these produce a sugary liquid called nectar, which the insects like to feed on. Bees and other insects have long tongues they use to suck up the nectar.

Butterfly tongue

If you watch a butterfly carefully when it is feeding, you can see the long tongue. It is coiled up under the head at other times but, for feeding, it uncoils to form a long tube.

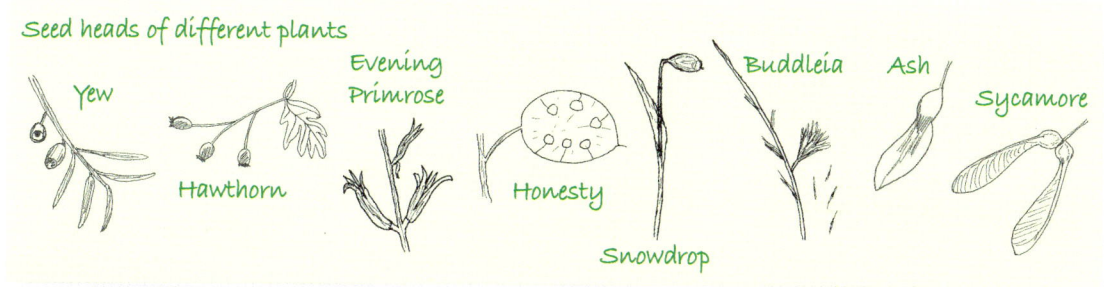

Seed heads of different plants: Yew, Hawthorn, Evening Primrose, Honesty, Snowdrop, Buddleia, Ash, Sycamore

> **So why are Large White butterflies attracted to cabbages that have no flowers?**

They land on them to lay their yellow eggs on the leaves. You can see these if you look carefully. After the small caterpillars hatch they feed on the cabbage leaf.

2 eggs of the Large White Butterfly on upperside of a cabbage leaf, and one newly hatched caterpillar eating the egg case

You see how one question leads on to lots of other questions and, if you keep on asking them, you can learn all about what goes on in your garden.

And you don't always have to ask someone else for the answer, or read a book; quite often you can work it out for yourself. To do this, you have to think of reasons *why* what you see is happening.

In other words, when you see things in the garden, you should ask, not only "What is it?" but "What is it doing?" Even for plants, instead of thinking "Well, they're not *doing* anything," you could ask the question we started with, "Why is it flowering?"

Here's another question.

> **Why do birds come into your garden?**

In some cases, in the spring, they arrive to nest.

How many birds nest in *your* garden?

The most likely would be Blackbirds and Song Thrushes which nest in bushes, Robins which nest in odd corners, often up against a wall, and Blue or Great Tits, especially if they can find a hole in a tree or a nest-box. In the spring, you may see them collecting nesting materials, twigs, moss, horse-hair, dried grass and, in the case of thrushes, mud to line the nest with.

But birds also come to feed.

Do you have a bird table?

If so, who visits that? Do some of the birds chase others off?

Blackbirds will visit the lawn to feed on earthworms. These are quite long worms (up to 10cm) and live in the soil, actually eating it as they make burrows. If you watch the Blackbirds you will see them holding their heads on one side. They are listening, and can suddenly dig out a worm because they heard it moving. Most animals have far better hearing than us, better eyesight and a better-developed sense of smell.

Song Thrushes are especially fond of snails and crack open the shells by banging them on a brick path or a special stone called an 'anvil', after the block that blacksmiths use to beat metal. You can often find a collection of broken shells where this happens.

Song thrush's "anvil" surrounded by opened shells

Birds also visit a garden for water and, if you have a pond, it is better to arrange a suitably shallow area so that they can drink safely – and also bathe.

Most birds are visitors, that is they rarely live in the garden but range over a much larger area.

So if we want birds to visit, you have to think carefully about why they would want to arrive in the first place.

If your garden has large trees, you may also see one of our three kinds of woodpeckers.

Two of them are called 'spotted' woodpeckers because of their black and white 'barred' colouring with a red head: one of them, the Great Spotted Woodpecker, is about the size of a thrush but the other, the Lesser Spotted Woodpecker, is much smaller, about the size of a sparrow.

In the early spring, you can hear them 'drumming', rapidly banging their beaks on the branches of big trees. They do this to tell their rivals that this is their patch of woodland. Then they dig out holes in the trees to nest in. Usually these are on the underside of branches (especially willow) so that the rain doesn't come in.

The largest of our woodpeckers – the Green Woodpecker – is about the size of a dove, rather smaller than a pigeon, and is bright green and yellow with a red crest.

All these woodpeckers have a 'dipping' flight.

The Green Woodpecker, or Yaffle, is commonly seen on the lawn, often with its beak pointed upwards. It is searching for ants, its favourite food – not the black garden ants but little yellow ones that live under the grass on the lawn.

The bird has a very long, sticky tongue and, after digging a small hole next to an ants' nest, it puts in its tongue to lick up the ants.

If you see a Green Woodpecker doing this, keep still or it will quickly fly away. When it has gone, go and look at the place where it was digging and you'll find the holes it made. Whenever you see such holes next to an ants' nest, you will be able to tell that a woodpecker has visited even if you don't see it anymore.

There are some small creatures in the garden you will probably never see unless you know where to look.

What's under stones and logs?

Small animals have to hide away in order to avoid being eaten or to prevent them from drying up in the sun, so you can find them under stones, loose bark or logs. The most common are

Woodlice
Centipedes and Millipedes
Small snails

Woodlice
These small animals have a hard, protective covering on the body, partly to avoid them drying out. That's why they like the damp soil under stones and logs. They are quite harmless and can easily be watched. They feed on dead plant matter.

How many legs do they have?

Remember all insects have six legs: so if they don't, they're not insects, are they?

Centipedes
Centipedes are usually brown – often quite a pale brown, nearly yellow and flat. They have many legs, one pair for each segment. The number of legs is very variable. Some centipedes have about 60 legs, for instance, and others well over a hundred.

See if you can count them. (A magnifying glass helps.) This is difficult because they move so fast; they do this because they are hunters, living on other small animals.

Millipedes
Millipedes tend to be grey/black and rounded. They are vegetarians and move slowly, so they need their protective hard outer coat. Like centipedes (centi = hundreds), millipedes also have many legs, in fact many more (milli = thousands), with two pairs to each segment.

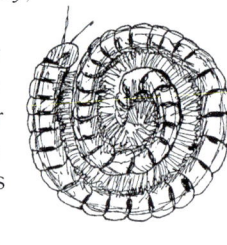

Snails
There are lots of different kinds of snails. Some are small and

flat and can easily fit under stones and logs. Others are larger and may be striped with black, brown and yellow rings – these are called banded snails. The most common garden snails are much larger – up to 3cm across – and need to find spaces big enough to crawl into.

What are ladybirds doing?

In summer you find them on rose bushes and other plants that have greenfly (also called aphids), because this is what ladybirds eat.

They usually lay yellow eggs on the leaf surface and when the 'larvae' hatch, these will also feed on greenfly.

7-spot ladybird

This is why gardeners like ladybirds. Greenfly damage plants by sucking up the plant sap and can also spread plant diseases.

Ladybird larva

In the winter, however, you will find ladybirds often crowded together in yew hedges, in sheds or in the cracks of your windowsill. This is where they overwinter until spring.

Ladybirds are easily identified by their bright orange or red colour and black spots. The most common are 2-spot and 7-spot ladybirds. However, there are many different kinds. Some are black with red spots, some yellow with black spots, and the number of spots may be 14 or even as high as 22. You may also find the much larger Harlequin ladybird, a recently introduced species, which is nearly as common as the 7-spot one.

How many different kinds can you find?

How many legs does a ladybird have? Is it an insect?

What's in the pond?

If you have lots of fish, there will probably be very few other creatures present such as little animals since the fish will eat them.

Some of the plants may be water lilies, which have lovely flowers and big, flat, floating leaves, and underwater plants like Canadian pondweed.

Small animals hide amongst these plants and some feed on them.

There are four main groups of small animals that you may see.
Pond snails
Pond skaters
Water lice
Dragonflies

Pond snails
There are two common snails, easily recognised, and both lay their eggs on the underside of lily leaves (if they have a choice).

Common Pond Snail (about 1cm)

Ramshorn Snail (about 3cm)

These eggs are readily found and you can soon tell them apart with a bit of practice. Both lay their eggs in a sort of clear jelly. The Common Pond Snail makes long, sausage-like tubes, whereas the Ramshorn Snail lays pinkish eggs in a flat mass of jelly.

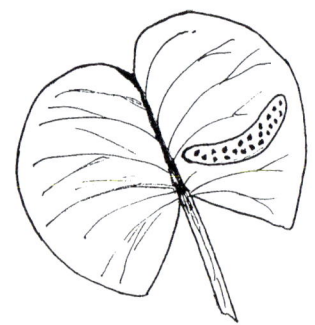

Eggs of Common Pond Snail

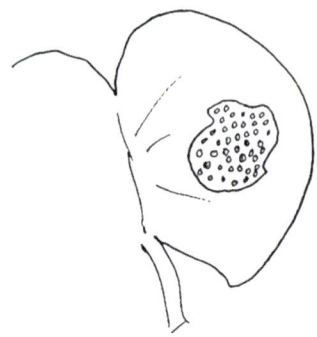

Eggs of Ramshorn Snail

Because the jelly is transparent, you can actually see the eggs hatching and the baby snails developing.

The adults grow up to 2cm across, but the newly-hatched babies, once they leave the lily leaf, are very hard to see.

The snails feed on small plants called 'algae' that give the green colour on the sides of ponds and glass in an aquarium. They 'graze' on these plants by scraping them with their tongues which are covered in tiny, very hard teeth.

Pond skaters
These are insects which 'skate' about on the surface of the water, feeding on smaller insects that fall into the water.

How do you think they manage to walk on water without getting wet?

Look carefully at their legs. First of all, these are long and spread the weight of the insect.

Secondly, they end in special feet with hairs that prevent them breaking the surface.

Water lice
Like the woodlice you find under stones, water lice also feed on dead plants. They are slow moving, and are protected by their hard covering. They don't swim but crawl slowly along the mud at the bottom.

Dragonflies
These spectacular, often brightly-coloured insects are expert fliers, with big eyes, and zoom about over the water, catching their food.

Dragonfly with wings spread out at rest

But you can also watch them dipping down when they lay their eggs into the water. These are tiny and too small for you to see, but fierce little youngsters hatch from them that live for up to three years in the water, eating other small animals, including insects. Adults only live for a few weeks.

Dragonflies are quite big but there are also smaller damselflies. Here you see a damselfly laying eggs into water with the male adult still clasping the female.

Wings folded over body

Finally, here's a different sort of question.

What would you like to have in your garden?

Different plants?

More butterflies? What could you do to attract them?

A pond – with or without fish?

More trees – with a tree-house?

What about paths?

Would you go to the trouble of putting down some logs or flat stones to look under?

What about nest boxes, a bird table or bird bath?

Why not try to draw the garden you would like to have?

And, in your present garden, why not try drawing the things you find?

Butterflies and Moths

Can you tell the difference between a butterfly and a moth?

Butterflies are out during the daytime; moths come out at night – but not all.

Butterflies usually rest with their wings folded above their backs.

Peacock butterfly

This has the advantage of hiding the brightly coloured upper parts of their wings, so that birds, which eat them, are less likely to see them when they're not flying. Moths rest with their wings stretched out.

Many butterflies are brightly coloured, whereas moths are mostly pale cream or brown, although some, especially day-flying ones, can be very colourful.

Do you know what causes the colour on their wings?

The wings are covered in tiny scales (about 0.1 mm in length) and these reflect the light in different ways, producing the colours.

Scales from the wings of a butterfly (greatly magnified)

Isn't it amazing that butterflies of one species seem to have exactly the same pattern of colours as all the other members of that species?

In the winter, some butterflies overwinter in this country by hiding in sheds and houses and many of them die, often because they emerge too soon, fooled by a warm day into thinking that spring has arrived.

In my cottage as many as a dozen may do this; you just find them dead or flapping about. It doesn't really help to put them outside because it is usually too cold for them.

Anyway, if you find a dead one you can touch the wings and the scales will come off on your finger. You could look at them through a magnifying glass.

This is also a good time to look at their 'feelers' or antennae. In most butterflies these end in knobs, whereas in moths the antennae are often feathery and don't have knobs.

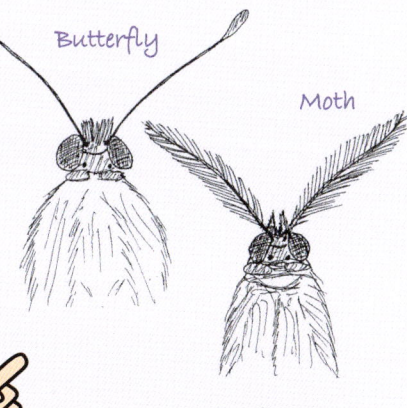

Butterfly

Moth

The earliest butterflies to appear in the spring are the ones that overwinter in this country.

The Small Tortoiseshell is one; others include the Peacock butterfly, which has big 'eyes' on its wings and the Brimstone, which hibernates in evergreen bushes and ivy. Only the upper surfaces of the male Brimstone butterflies' wings are bright yellow, the undersides are green, so it blends well with the leaves of the bushes. The female is a paler yellowy-green all over.

Brimstone butterfly

Other butterflies, like the Red Admiral, the Painted Lady and the Comma are more common in gardens in the autumn – from August onwards. They can be found feeding on Buddleia and later on ripe plums and fallen fruit.

Comma butterfly

Butterflies and moths come to the garden for two reasons – either to feed or to lay eggs.

Butterflies drinking

They only feed on liquids, mostly from flowers with lots of nectar; some butterflies may also drink at muddy puddles; this is not so much for the water as for the minerals dissolved in it.

Their tongues are quite remarkable. They are actually in two parts that fit together to form a tube; this is coiled up under the head when not in use.

Because caterpillars can't travel far, the eggs have to be placed on the plant they're going to feed on. The Small Tortoiseshell and Peacock use the Stinging Nettle for egg laying. This grows quite early in the spring and the eggs are laid on the new shoots. The caterpillars of the two species are easy to tell apart.

Small Tortoiseshell caterpillars are rather bristly and black and green in colour, whereas the caterpillars of the Peacock butterfly are velvety black.

There are many more sorts of moths than butterflies. You don't see them much because most come out at night. They are attracted to light however, so you may see them crowding round lamps or appearing at lighted windows.

An easily recognised moth caterpillar is the 'Woolly Bear', orange and black and very hairy. It is actually the caterpillar of the Garden Tiger Moth, quite a brightly coloured one, alas now rather rare.

It is worth remembering that the hairs on hairy caterpillars can irritate the skin and so you should never put your fingers near your eyes if you have been handling them.

How do you suppose caterpillars change into adult butterflies or moths?

After all, they look completely different, don't they?

In fact, there's hardly anything the same between them, except that they all have six legs.

Even this is confused by the fact that caterpillars may also have some stumpy false legs at their rear end whilst the proper legs are at the front, just behind the head.

So caterpillars don't just grow into butterflies or moths, they have to be completely changed.

They do this by 'pupating'. This means forming a hard – usually brown and often shiny – case called a 'pupa'. Most of them are rather barrel-shaped. Before a caterpillar changes into a pupa it seeks out a protected place where it can safely rest for some time, often over winter.

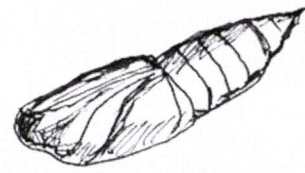

Moth pupa

Many moth caterpillars pupate in the soil. Butterfly caterpillars usually hang downwards, suspended by a silken thread against a wall, in a shed or some other sheltered spot, but sometimes they are the right way up.

Then, inside this pupal case, the whole body is reorganised to form the adult.

Isn't this extraordinary?

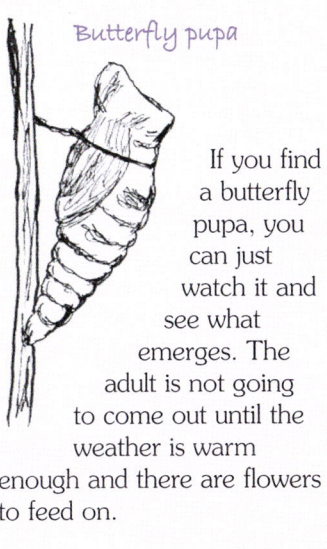

Butterfly pupa

If you find a butterfly pupa, you can just watch it and see what emerges. The adult is not going to come out until the weather is warm enough and there are flowers to feed on.

If you find a moth pupa – for instance when you are digging in the garden – you can keep it in some soil in a fairly cool place until the adult moth emerges. Then you can try and identify it – there are books to tell you how to do that.

Eye on wing of Purple Emperor

Bees, Wasps and Ants

Bees

There are different sorts of bees. I am sure you will have seen honeybees and bumblebees in your garden, which look quite different from each other. Both kinds of bees live in family groups.

Honeybees are kept by people in special big wooden boxes, called 'hives', where they live, rear their young and store honey – and that's mainly why people keep them, to get the honey.

↳ Actual size

If you watch honeybees in the garden, you will see that they spend time visiting flowers.

Why do you think they do this?

There are two reasons: They suck up the nectar, a sugary liquid, and make it into honey in their hives to store it as food, but they also collect pollen, rich in protein, mostly to feed their young, called larvae or grubs. These hatched out of eggs to eventually turn into adult bees.

Why do you think flowers produce nectar for bees and other small animals that visit?

Flowers make pollen, and the pollen has to be moved to other flowers where it helps to make the seeds (this is called pollination) – and you need seeds to grow more flowers.

Now the pollen can't move by itself, but when bees visit to get nectar, they become dusted with pollen which they then carry on their furry coats to another flower and pollinate it. Of course, bees also collect the pollen, which they feed to their grubs. They store it in special 'baskets' on their hind legs, so that they can carry it whilst flying away. You can easily see these bright yellow baskets of pollen.

Hindlegs of a bumblebee

empty pollenbasket

Pollen in pollenbasket

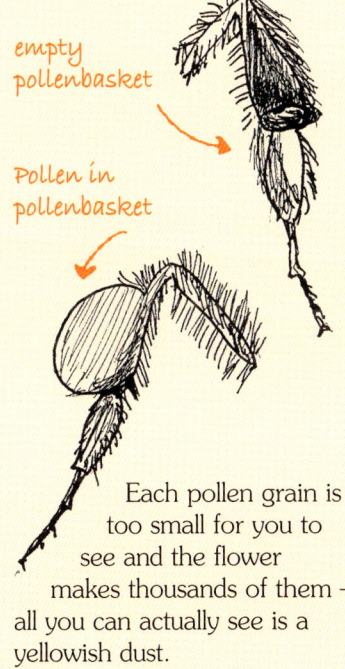

Each pollen grain is too small for you to see and the flower makes thousands of them – all you can actually see is a yellowish dust.

Some plants flower in very early spring when few bees or other pollinating insects are about, so how do they manage to become pollinated?

How do bees make honey?

Honey is made entirely from nectar and, because different plants produce quite different sorts of nectar, several quite different kinds of honey result.

The main task in making honey is to reduce, by evaporation, the high water content of nectar. The bees that collect the nectar do this by regurgitating it (that is, bringing it up from their "honey stomachs") and pushing their tongues in and out through it repeatedly – about 90 times!

After the "unripe honey" has been put in a wax cell in the hive, "house bees" repeat the process until about 15% of the water has been lost. The honey is then stored in a cell.

The answer is that they use the wind. The flowers with the pollen are often catkins that hang down so that the wind can blow the pollen about.

Silver birch catkins

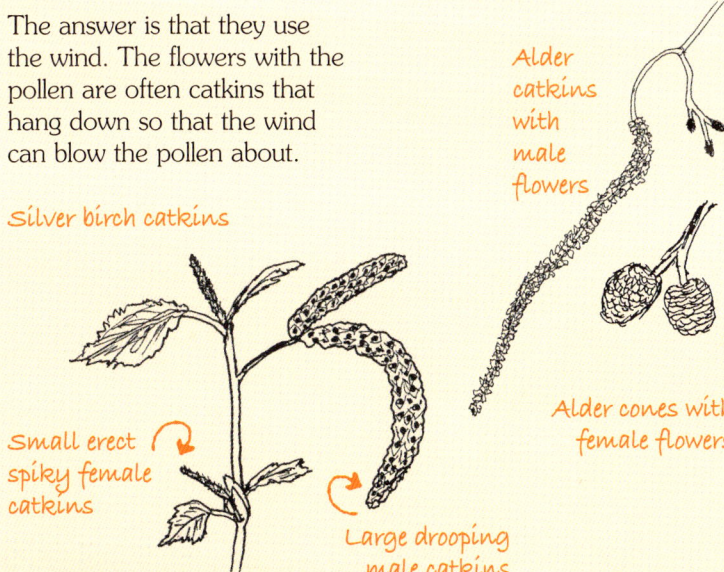

Small erect spiky female catkins

Large drooping male catkins

Alder catkins with male flowers

Alder cones with female flowers

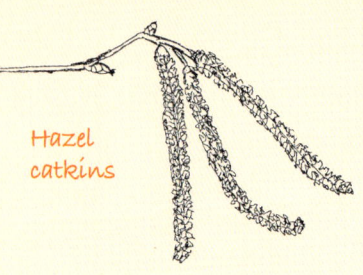

Hazel catkins

You can see catkins on hazel bushes that later produce hazel nuts or on bushes of 'pussy willow'. These catkins are covered in bright silvery hairs and appear in January or February. Blue tits will sometimes land on them to eat the pollen.

> Do you know why the bush is called a pussy willow?

Pussy Willow catkins

It's because it has 'cat-kins' – little cats.

You will only see one sort of honeybee, but there will be hundreds, sometimes many thousands, of them in each hive.

Bumblebees are much bigger and there are many different kinds.

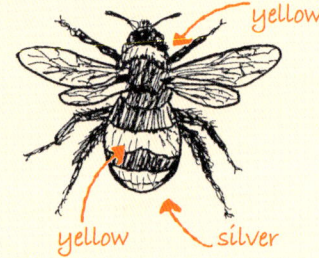

Actual size

Queen Bumblebee

yellow *yellow* *silver*

If you look carefully at them you will see that most have yellow and silver bands across the abdomen, as shown in the drawing. Not all bumblebees have the same coloured bands. See if you can spot some different kinds.

One of the largest bumblebees to be found in Britain doesn't have such bands but rather has a reddish-orange tail and is called the Red-tailed Bumblebee.

Although they are so much bigger than honeybees, and can sting, they are much less likely to sting you unless you disturb their nests.

Most bumblebees nest underground, usually in an old mouse-hole, but there are two kinds that make a nest of moss above ground. This is about 10cm across and contains cells made of wax in which the larvae are reared.

Although honey- and bumblebees both live in family groups, bumblebee families are much smaller and often have only about 20 members, compared with the big colonies of honeybees.

Much less noticeable are lots of different kinds of bees that do not live in groups – the so-called *solitary bees*. They are all much smaller and most dig little tunnels in the ground, where each female lays its eggs. Unless you are looking for them, you probably won't see them at all, but you should keep an eye out for them. They are very interesting insects indeed.

Wasps

> Why do you think wasps are so brightly coloured?

It warns you that they are dangerous, and indeed wasp stings are very painful. When a bee stings you, it leaves the sting in your flesh and results in the death of the bee. But a wasp can sting several times.

European Wasp

Usually wasps only sting when they are attacked – or when they think they're being attacked. And this may happen when you accidentally disturb them or, worse still, their nests.

Very often they nest underground, using old nests of mice for example and will enlarge them to a big space, perhaps more than 30cm across. During this time, you can see them as they come out of the tunnel entrance, each carrying a little crumb of soil. They fly away with it and drop it quite a long way off, so that the nest entrance is not given away to would-be predators by the presence of a heap of soil.

Quite often wasps nest in lofts and attics. There you can see their amazing nests made entirely of paper!

If you see a wasp sitting on a fence post or a dead tree, it can often be seen scraping tiny wood shavings off. It then chews this to produce wood pulp which it uses to build the nest, spreading it in very thin layers. These layers are so thin that they fall apart in your hand. But they are strong enough for the wasps to make little six-sided cells in which they lay their eggs and rear their young.

A wasp nest may contain hundreds of wasps, so it is dangerous to disturb them.

Big wasps' nest, found in my attic!

Shows the layers of cells in the wasps' nest

Shows the paper pillars supporting each layer

Probably even more dangerous is a much larger kind of wasp called a **Hornet**. It is brown and yellow and can sometimes be very fierce. Its sting is said to be much worse than that of a wasp.

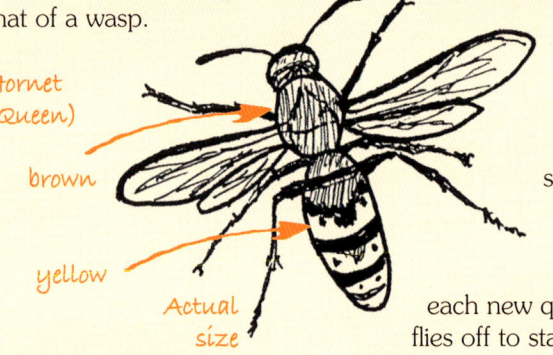

Hornet (Queen)
brown
yellow
Actual size

So never disturb Hornets – you can tell them by their size and colour. Just as with bees, there are many different kinds of wasp that do not live in groups but live on their own. And, just like the bees, they are quite small and often make tunnels in the soil. Wasps don't collect pollen but feed their young on other insects which they catch while out hunting.

Wasps also like sugary liquids, which is why they can bother you on a picnic. They love jam especially.

Ants

Ants also live in large family groups or colonies and as with honey bees and wasps, each colony has a queen, the head of the family, which lays all the eggs. When the colony gets too big, some of the eggs hatch into new queens, and each new queen then flies off to start a new colony of its own.

Ants differ from bees and wasps in one major way. You will notice that, whereas all bees and wasps have wings, ants don't – at least, that is, most of the ants you see don't have wings most of the time. They do live underground and they dig tunnels in the soil and make 'rooms' where they rear their young.

But on hot summer days, quite suddenly, a swarm of winged ants may appear. There will be hundreds of them, and people worry because they sometimes come into the house. There's nothing to worry about; the whole thing only lasts one day and the winged forms are quite harmless.

The reason for all this is that the new queens, which have wings, fly off along with many winged males to set up a new home and colony. Once landed, they shed their glistening wings.

The honey bee queen also flies off with many other bees – a swarm – to a new nest site. Wasp queens don't swarm.

Yellow ant's hills

In the common wasp – those yellow and black ones that forage for sweet things as well as meat – only the queens survive the winter, whilst all the other wasps die as soon as winter sets in. In contrast, all the family members of bees and ants, including the queen, do overwinter.

Have you noticed that, even though ants look very similar, they often differ in size and colour?

See how many kinds you can find.

The most common are black and they often live under flat stones, sometimes in footpaths.

Also very common, but not so easily seen, are yellow ants. These usually live under the lawn. If the grass is not cut for a couple of weeks, they may start to build nests above the ground and little heaps of soil appear.

Of course, these are flattened next time the grass is cut, but if an area is left uncut and allowed to become rough grass, these heaps can become very large, sometimes 60cm long and 30cm high!

There are also red ants and they, too, build mounds of earth, but they are not so big.

And there are tiny black ants, often called 'honey' ants that come into our houses, especially the kitchen or larder if food has been spilt.

Most ants feed on other insects but lots of them like sweet things. This is why some kinds of ants, including the most common black ant, can be found farming greenfly on plants.

When greenfly suck the sap from the plant, they produce drops of sugary liquid called 'honey dew' which the ants eat

Ants feeding on honey dew of aphids

In exchange for this, the ants protect the greenfly from insects that would normally eat them, including the ladybirds. So both ants and greenfly benefit from each other.

Nests

Probably when you think of nests you immediately think of birds' nests. But lots of other animals make nests too – bumblebees, for example.

Why do animals build nests?

With birds, of course, the answer is easy – to lay their eggs in. All garden birds do, although in the case of pigeons this is usually a platform of twigs in the branches of a tree. And in fact, some birds don't build nests at all. Certain seabirds just lay their eggs on a rocky ledge.

But why, you might ask, do birds need nests to lay eggs in?

One good reason for a nest is to put the eggs out of reach of those who would eat them – predators.

Do you know who might do this?

The most common egg-stealers are Grey Squirrels, Magpies and Jays. These last two are big birds and small birds cannot usually adequately defend their eggs.

Magpie eyeing duck eggs

So they want to hide them. This is why so many eggs are coloured or speckled – it makes them more difficult to see. (This is called 'camouflage': soldiers do the same with uniforms that are hard to make out in the field.)

The eggs are even harder to spot when the mother is sitting on them! Mostly it is the mother bird, called a hen, that does this, but a few hen birds share this job with the cock or male bird.

Since it is mostly the hen that sits on the eggs, she is usually much less brightly coloured than the cock bird. Have a look at chaffinches, bullfinches, ducks and drakes, even blackbirds, and you will see the difference between the sexes.

What about robins and thrushes?

Here the hens and cocks are the same in appearance but the colour (or the speckled part in thrushes) is only on the breast, so you can't see it when the bird is sitting on the nest.

With big birds, like jays and magpies, there is no need to look different, partly because they can defend their nests. In addition, magpies actually have a roof on their nests, the only big birds to do so, built near the tops of bushes or trees.

Why are so many birds' nests found in bushes, trees or high up like walls?

One reason is that a lot of the predators, like snakes, foxes, rats and mice, that would eat bird eggs, don't generally climb trees.

So nests are safer higher up. Some small birds, such as Hedge Sparrows, often build their nests at the end of long branches, so that heavier animals, like squirrels, can't get at them – the branches are not strong enough to support their weight.

Robins nest in very odd places, such as on top of a post against a wall or even inside an old teapot!

Wrens, too, like odd places, in corners just under a shed roof or lodged in the ivy covering a tree trunk. It is interesting that only the male builds the nest; he builds several, 2 or 3, and lets the female choose which one to lay her eggs in. You can always tell a wren's nest because it has a roof on it.

A magpie's nest: it has a roof and the birds get in through the side

Nest of a wren

33

Best-protected nests are those built by House Martins. Perhaps your house has some of their nests?

They are made of mud mixed with birds' saliva and some plant fibres, which, when dry, makes very hard pellets. They stick these together under the eaves – where the roof overhangs the walls. Each nest has only a small entrance and can easily be defended, although only another bird could reach the nest anyway. These mud-cups are lined with dried grass and feathers.

House martin feeding their young in nest

All these various types of nests also serve as nurseries for the young when they hatch from the egg and for several weeks whilst they are growing up.

Not many garden birds nest on the ground but, in large gardens, pheasants for example and water birds do. Pheasants only make a rough hollow amongst dead leaves and grass.

Ducks, moorhens and coots nest at ground level often where they are surrounded by water. So foxes and squirrels can't reach them, but big predatory birds can. However, these nests are usually so placed that they are hard to find. Before ducks go off to feed, they cover up their eggs with leaves.

When the eggs hatch, the young leave the nest within a day or two and swim with their parents. They are able to do this because they are well developed, their eyes are open and they are covered with waterproof down.

Nest of a Mallard duck with eggs

Perching birds, like the robins, are quite different: when their eggs hatch, the young are helpless, with no feathers and their eyes shut. So they have to be fed all the time, and the parents are kept very busy finding enough food for them.

In most cases, because of all this landing and taking off by the parents and by the increasing movements of the young, the nest does not last long after they have left and a new one has to be built the next year.

Some birds, with nests built of stout twigs and small branches, use the same nest from year to year, simply repairing any damage or adding to it. Rooks generally do this and crows sometimes do.

Strangely enough, most of the birds that make holes in trees, such as the woodpeckers, make a new hole each year; perhaps because by doing so, they escape from parasitic insects like fleas.

The holes, of course, remain there for years and get used by other birds, including Starlings and Blue and Great Tits. They line the holes to make them more comfortable and may also use them from year to year.

House Martins will actually return from overwintering thousands of miles away in South Africa to the same nest each year.

What other creatures do nest in trees and bushes?

The main ones are squirrels, although dormice make nests in bushes, where they also spend the winter.

Squirrels make quite bulky nests, called 'dreys', usually near the tops of trees but sometimes in a hollow tree or a cleft between the branches and the trunk.

These dreys are made mainly of small branches with dead leaves and are just a big bundle of them with a hollow chamber in the middle, often lined with dried leaves and ivy.

Wasps and hornets may also nest in hollow trees.

As mentioned earlier, bumblebees that nest above ground make their nests mainly of moss. These look very similar to those of voles and are found in similar places (in long grass).

Squirrel's drey

Vole's nest: a bumblebees' nest looks just like this but without the entrance hole

A Field vole in front of its nest

The entrance to a rabbit's burrow, showing the earth that has been dug out

The entrance to a badger sett under a dead oak tree.

Wood mice also make these kinds of nests if they find a protected spot; otherwise they nest in holes in the ground.

Many animals make their homes underground, where they are protected from the weather and, to some extent, from predators.

Rabbits are the most noticeable, the entrance to their burrows being readily seen and often marked by a long trail of soil they have dug out.

Badgers also take no trouble to hide their enormous homes called 'setts', because they have few enemies. Many badgers will set up house together, often in a wooded bank, with many entrances and also, in the early spring, with great piles of soil near them.

Quite often, rabbits and badgers have a 'spring-cleaning' and clear out all the old bedding, probably to get rid of fleas and ticks. Badgers are hard to see, because they are very shy and come out at night.

But rabbits can be seen during the day collecting dried grass and other vegetation, scraping it backwards to tuck it under their chins (they often look as though they've got a moustache!), and taking it down the burrow for new bedding.

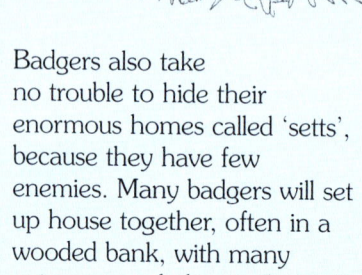

Rabbit taking bedding into its burrow

Of course, we don't usually call these holes in the ground 'nests' and that's why many people think of nests as being made by birds to lay their eggs in.

But other animals lay eggs and don't build nests.

Can you think of any?

Snakes are one example. The Grass Snake, our most common snake, lays quite a lot of eggs – about 30-40. They are rather leathery and don't have hard shells as the eggs of birds do.

However, they don't just leave them anywhere; they find a heap of vegetation in which to hide them. Their favourite places are a compost heap or a heap of fresh grass cuttings. This is because these heaps get quite warm as the leaves are broken down by microbes, which helps the development of the snake embryos.

Try putting a heap of grass cuttings together and, after an hour or two, feel how warm it gets inside. You'll be surprised, because it gets hotter than you would expect.

A Grass Snake, found under a dustbin lid

So it's not really a nest, which is made by the animal, but it serves a similar purpose. However, unlike birds, the snake shows no interest in the eggs once they have been laid – it just leaves them where they are and lets the warmth do the rest.

So, one of the things all birds do is look after the eggs and the young when they hatch.

Now, most insects lay eggs: do you think they look after them?

Most do not, although the earwig does.

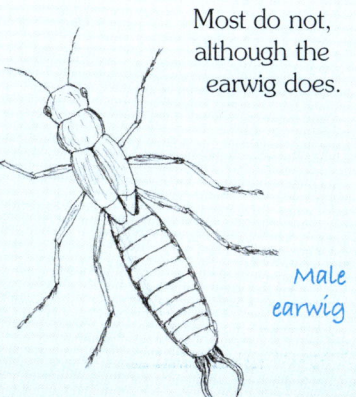

Male earwig

Enlarged pincers of female earwig

The female earwig lays its eggs in a little pit in the soil, keeps them clean by licking them and sits on top of them until they hatch in the spring. After that, she stays to feed them for the first part of their lives and also guards them from predators, attacking any would-be enemies with her pincers.

Do you think any other animals lay eggs and look after them?

Surprisingly two other creatures look after their young – spiders and sticklebacks.

Several spiders can be seen in long grass scuttling about, carrying their bundles of eggs – so-called egg sacs – either on their backs or attached behind them. The wolf spider carries its eggs in a silken cocoon at the end of its body and, when they hatch, may carry the young on its back for a while.

But some build cone-shaped spider webs to form a kind of tent.

Wolf spider with eggsac

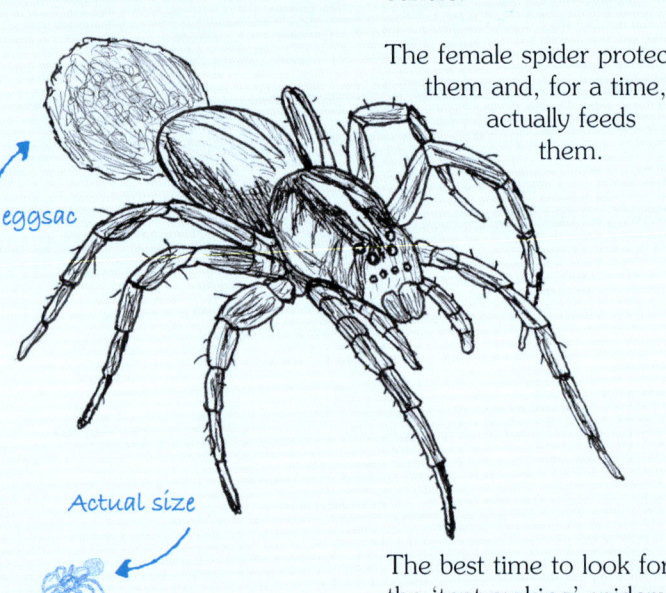

eggsac

Actual size

They lay their eggs inside and when these hatch, the tiny spiderlings stay together for several days. You can see them inside their 'tents' and watch them gradually spread out as they get bolder.

Then, when they are alarmed, for example by you gently tapping the tent, they all rush together again, forming a closely packed bundle.

The female spider protects them and, for a time, actually feeds them.

The best time to look for the 'tent-making' spiders is June and they may only have their nests and young over a period of a few weeks. Just like most birds, they only build nests and rear their young for a part of the year, mostly in the spring.

Spider building tent-like web

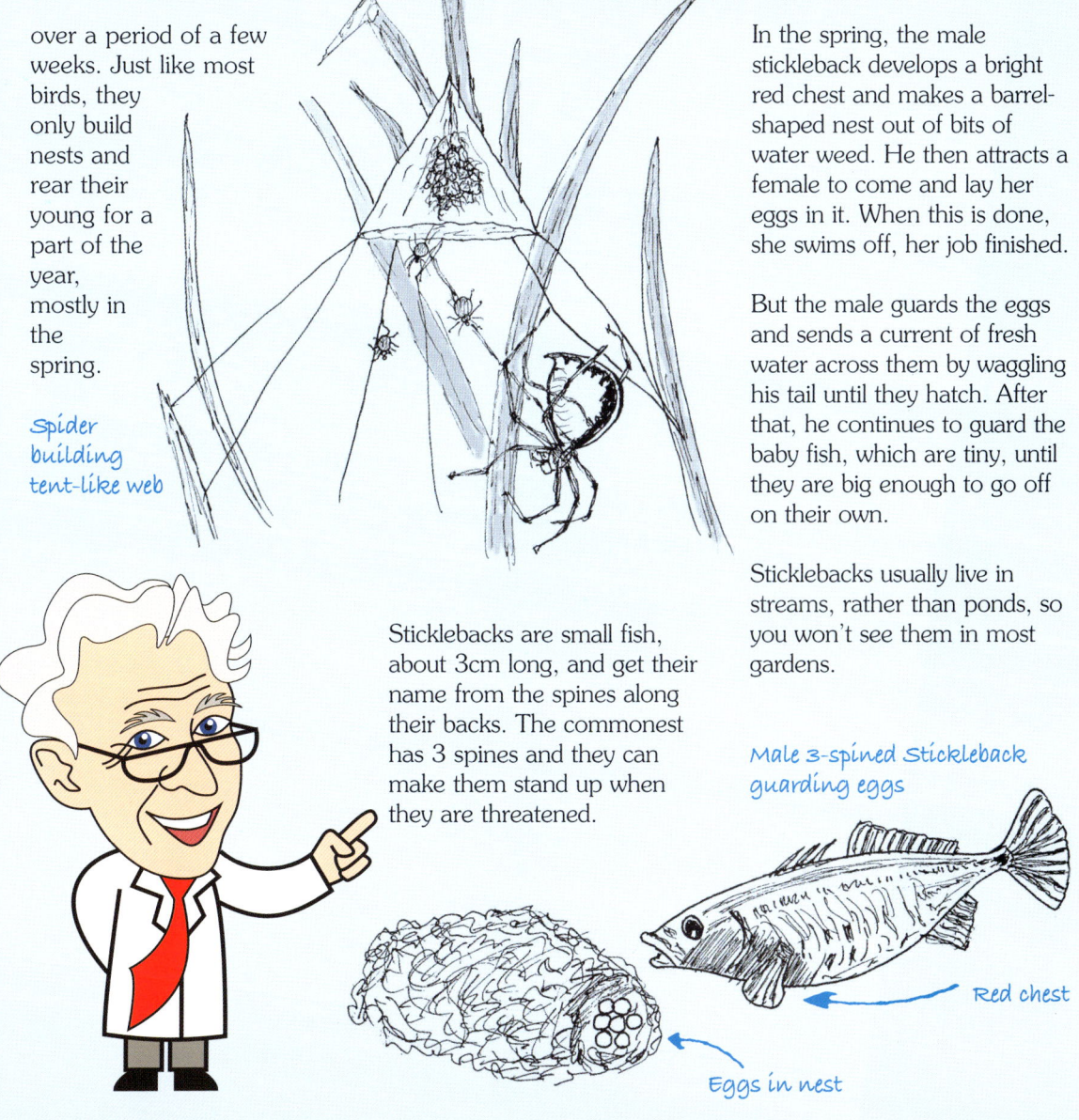

Sticklebacks are small fish, about 3cm long, and get their name from the spines along their backs. The commonest has 3 spines and they can make them stand up when they are threatened.

In the spring, the male stickleback develops a bright red chest and makes a barrel-shaped nest out of bits of water weed. He then attracts a female to come and lay her eggs in it. When this is done, she swims off, her job finished.

But the male guards the eggs and sends a current of fresh water across them by waggling his tail until they hatch. After that, he continues to guard the baby fish, which are tiny, until they are big enough to go off on their own.

Sticklebacks usually live in streams, rather than ponds, so you won't see them in most gardens.

Male 3-spined Stickleback guarding eggs

Red chest

Eggs in nest

Eggs

Why do animals produce eggs?

Do all of them?

Many animals give birth to live young – dogs, cats, people, rabbits, foxes, mice and hedgehogs, for example.

This means that the mother has to carry them around inside her until they are ready to be born, with all their legs, eyes, head and body quite well grown. This can take a long time: the bigger the animal, the longer it takes.

In contrast, laying eggs is much simpler and they can be produced quickly and in large numbers.

A duck, like a Mallard for example, may lay as many as 12 large eggs which will eventually hatch to produce a dozen fluffy ducklings. But now imagine this bird, instead of laying eggs, giving birth to 12 *live* ducklings!...

Furthermore, not all eggs are laid on one day, in the same way as a dog has puppies or a cat has kittens. Rather they are laid one a day and not necessarily every day. Several clutches may be laid per year.

So laying eggs seems to be much simpler and more young can be produced. On the other hand, bird eggs usually have to be sat on (incubated) to keep them warm until they hatch. And then the hatchlings may have to be fed for several weeks, until they can look after themselves.

Now, birds' eggs are roughly the same shape (egg-shaped!), like a hen's egg, yet they vary greatly in size and colour.

Mallard duck with ducklings

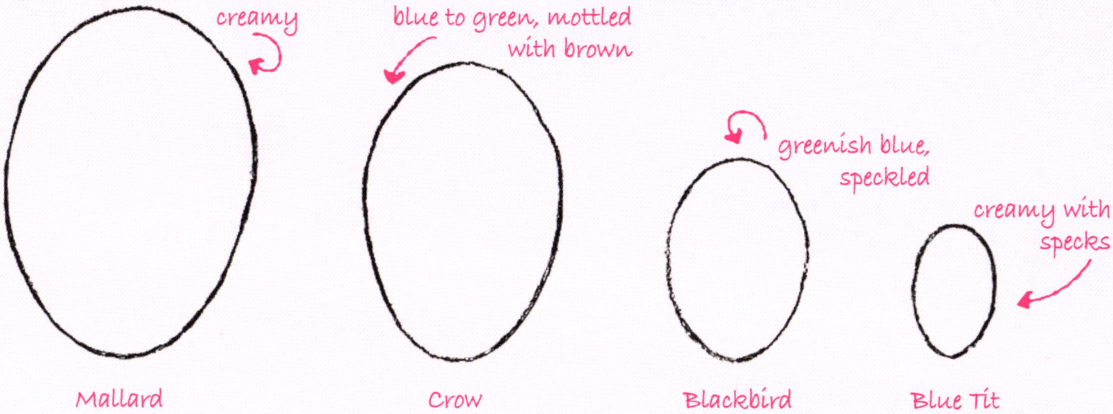

Mallard — creamy

Crow — blue to green, mottled with brown

Blackbird — greenish blue, speckled

Blue Tit — creamy with specks

Obviously, bigger birds will have bigger eggs but why do they differ in shape and colour?

For example the eggs of the Tawny Owl and the Great Spotted Woodpecker seem to be more round and both white.

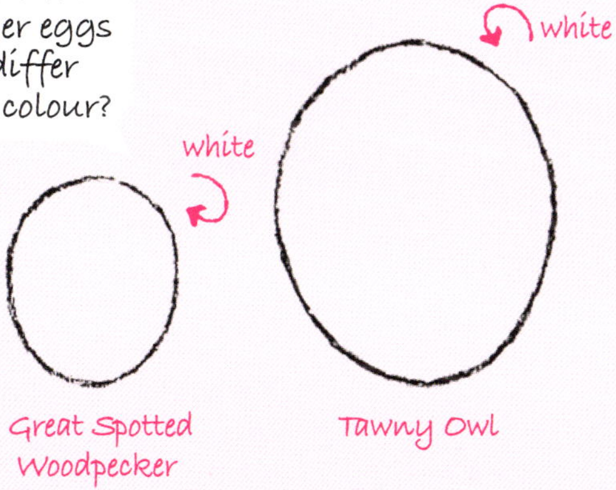

Great Spotted Woodpecker — white

Tawny Owl — white

Robin's nest with eggs

Sometimes, the shape is useful in packing them neatly in the nest but they also have to be easy to lay! No animal would want to lay a square-shaped egg, would it?

Colour helps to make the eggs more difficult to see, they are camouflaged: dots and blotches help to break up the outline. I wonder why there are no striped eggs – can you think of a reason?

When the eggs are white, with no colour pattern, they are either laid inside a tree trunk (in woodpecker holes, for example) or in nests that are well hidden or covered with leaves when the bird is away from the nest; ducks do this.

Which other animals lay eggs?

Many insects, but also toads and frogs (you will have seen frogspawn, I expect), newts, grass snakes and fish.

Insect eggs are, of course, quite small, but often produced in large numbers. They come in all sorts of shapes; some even have stalks, especially those of the lacewing flies.

Lacewing fly

Usually, the eggs are creamy-white or yellow. So they can manage without camouflage.

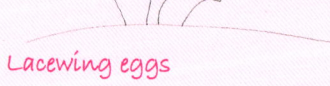

Lacewing eggs

This barrel-shaped egg with ridges is from the butterfly the Painted Lady. They are first light green and turn grey. They are laid on several different wild flowers.

The eggs of the Large White are very similar to those of the Small White; again they are barrel-shaped with ridges, but longish. In both cases they are first bright yellow but turn creamy later and are laid on leaves of cabbages.

The eggs of houseflies are white with a smooth surface; they almost look like small grains of rice. They are laid on meat or carcases of animals.

The female of the Lackey Moth lays the eggs in spirals around twigs and branches of trees and shrubs.

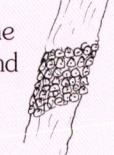

Eggs of the Lackey Moth

Most insects lay their eggs and leave the young to look after themselves. To make sure that they have enough food, eggs are laid on or very near a suitable food supply.

The freshly-hatched caterpillars of the Large White butterfly find plenty to eat.

Where the food is a plant, the eggs are laid on the leaves or stems, usually on the underside of the leaves. Why do they do this?

Since plants do not grow at all times of the year, insects usually lay their eggs in the spring, but some lay them in the autumn and the eggs overwinter. In this case the eggs are tough and are laid in protected spots such as crevices in the bark.

If the food of the young insects is not plant but animal – often little insects, for example – then the eggs are laid where such other insects are to be found. This may be under bark or under logs, where lots of small creatures gather.

Ladybirds eat greenfly, so they lay their eggs on the plants that the greenfly live on and, if possible, near to the greenfly themselves.

Snails and slugs lay creamy-white, round eggs, a bit bigger than those of insects. They can be found most often under logs and stones, often in little clumps of ten or more, or buried just under the soil.

They need to be kept moist, to stop them drying out and shrivelling up, but not wet because they might go mouldy.

Apart from birds' eggs, the ones you probably know best are those of the frog – the familiar frogspawn. This is a mass of jelly that floats in the water and is made up of hundreds of eggs. They look like black dots and each one is surrounded by clear jelly, which protects it from large insects and fish. It doesn't quite protect it from ducks, which seem to swallow the eggs, jelly and all.

However, because the jelly is so bulky (it swells up in the water after the frog produces it – otherwise the frog would have to be enormous!), a duck can only eat some of it. After all, some of the patches of frogspawn are as big as a duck.

Toads do much the same thing, but their eggs come out in a double chain which they wind round waterweed.

Frogspawn

Toadspawn

Other interesting things to think about:

In pet shops, you can often find so-called 'ants' eggs' for sale, as food for fish. However, if you look at these 'ants' eggs' you will see that they are as big as ants!

How could an ant lay an egg as big as itself?

If you look inside one (they are easy to open because they are a bit like tissue paper), you will find a whole (dead) ant.

Now real ants' eggs hatch into little white grubs (ant larvae) and when these have finished growing they make a little sausage-shaped, papery case, inside which the pupae turn into adult ants.

So these 'ants' eggs' are not eggs at all but are in fact ant pupae. The real eggs are much smaller and whitish, about the size of an ant's head.

43

Red ants with their white eggs found under dustbin lid

Eggshells

What do you think happens to all the eggshells in the spring, when lots of garden birds are hatching their eggs?

The birds don't want them cluttering up the nest but they don't want to just tip them out. If they did that, predators would know where the nest was, just by looking for a heap of eggshells on the ground.

Most birds carry them away from the nest and drop them some distance away. This is why you occasionally find eggshells in the middle of your lawn.

Newts have a very special way of laying their eggs. Each egg is laid singly and usually wrapped in the leaf of a waterweed.

Newt egg wrapped in a leaf

The female newt uses its hind feet to fold the leaf over the egg, which sticks it down in a little envelope. You can see inside the egg and, if you put some in a jam jar, you can watch the baby newt develop until it hatches. It eats very tiny little creatures so it is best to put it back in the pond, where it can find plenty to feed on.

Of course, other creatures also feed on the baby newts, especially the larvae of water beetles. They hide in the mud and in blanket weed – so this weed, often a nuisance to us in rivers and ponds, is very useful and important for these small animals!

If you disturb an ants' nest, you can see the ants carrying these eggs about in their jaws, moving them to a warmer or a cooler part of the nest at different times of day. This is to keep them at the best temperature for their development.

Hedges, Bushes and Trees

Hedges

Why do so many gardens have hedges?

Usually, the main reason is for privacy, to block out a busy road or ugly view. But also, like fences, they keep most pets in and other animals out. They also keep the wind at bay and so protect your house or your flowers in the garden.

What else are hedges good for?

They provide shelter for lots of small animals, and also provide food in terms of flowers and berries.

Birds like hedges because they are safe places to nest. In a thick hedge, the nest is well hidden; it is difficult for magpies and squirrels to get at them to steal eggs or even young birds.

Blackbirds, thrushes and robins are the most common birds to nest in hedges but lots of other small birds also do so.

Privet, yew and hawthorn make good hedges for birds to nest; they grow thick if cut regularly, and the hawthorn is also very prickly. Once established, they can grow very tall.

Also insects live or hide in them and wood mice live in the bottom of the hedge.

In wild hedges, lots of wild flowers grow at their base, especially shade-loving plants, like violets. Other plants use hedges to climb up, like bryony and bindweed.

Why do you think plants climb up other plants?

This is mainly to reach sunlight. Plants need light to grow. If you cover them up, they lose their green colour, get very thin and spindly and eventually die.

Climbing plants don't have stiff stems like most plants do and either need to climb up something else or flop about on the ground.

Have you seen peas and beans growing in the vegetable garden?

They have to have wooden stakes to grow up against.

Have you seen how they hold on to the stakes?

They have little curly bits called 'tendrils'. These reach out and when they touch something, twist round it, like vetches do in long grass and passion flowers along their supports.

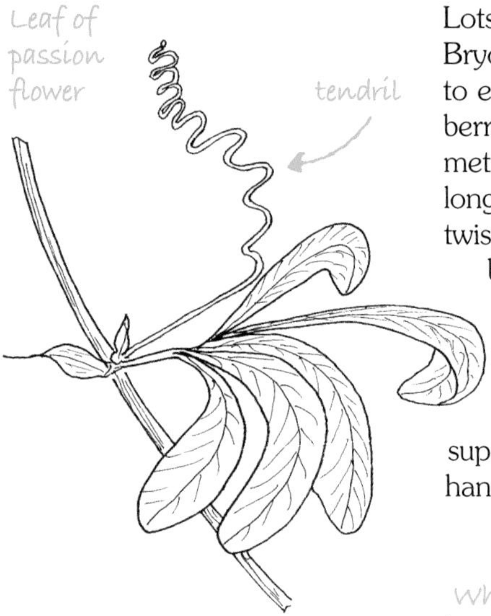

Leaf of passion flower

tendril

Lots of plants, like White Bryony (which is poisonous to eat, especially its red berries), can climb up several metres in this way with their long tendrils. These not only twist round part of the hedge but then make a coil, like a spring, that tightens as it grows. They like thick hedges because it is so easy to find support – lots of twigs to hang on to.

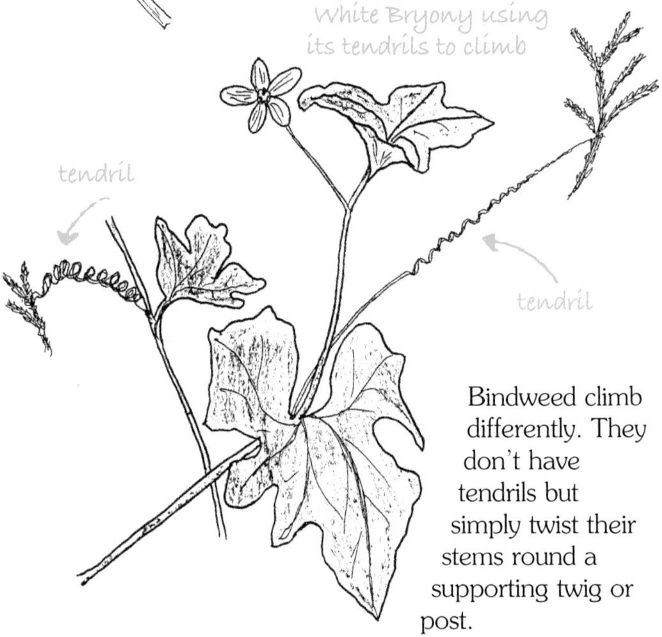

White Bryony using its tendrils to climb

tendril

tendril

Bindweed climb differently. They don't have tendrils but simply twist their stems round a supporting twig or post.

Leaf of vetch

flowers

tendril

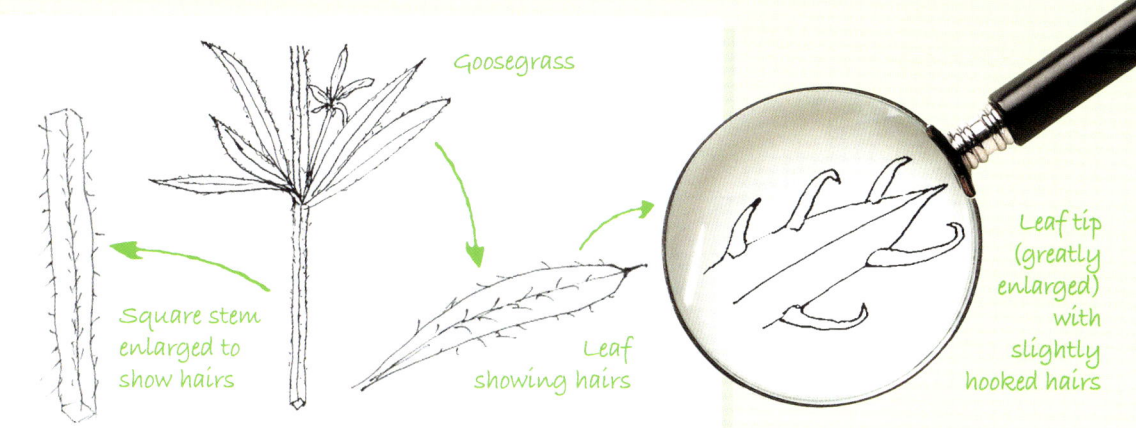

Cleavers or Goosegrass is also found in hedges. It is covered with little hairs, which stick to things (especially your clothes – quite harmless but difficult to pull off). These help the plant to climb.

You probably don't think of hedges as flowering, but they do. The flowers are an extra food source for many insects, and birds feed on seeds during the winter.

Some flowers are very small and therefore difficult to find. It helps to know what you are looking for. For example, I always have great trouble finding the male and female flowers of a yew hedge; see if you can do better. These grow on separate plants, and flower in late winter or early spring (remember that the leaves and fruits are very poisonous). In autumn, bright red/pink berries appear, a sort of cup with a seed in the middle.

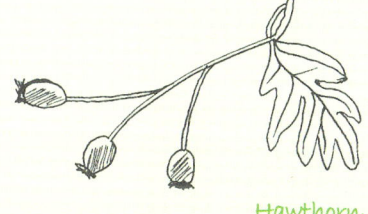

Flowers of hawthorn are much easier to see. They are creamy-white or reddish-pink – masses of them – that smell strongly. This is often called 'may' and appears in the spring. Later in the year these produce bunches of bright red berries.

Ivy hedges usually have quite big leaves – different from the ones that you find when it is climbing up walls or trees. The climbing sort sticks to the wall or to a tree trunk by means of tufts of little whitish roots, but in hedges the stems just twine round each other and can become quite thick.

The flowers are small and greenish – not very noticeable, but develop into bunches of green seedpods, each containing (usually) two seeds.

When birds eat any of these 'fruits' or seedpods, they digest the fleshy outer parts and the seeds themselves pass out in their droppings. So the seeds are spread all over the place as the birds fly about. Quite often, seeds won't develop at all if they have not passed through a bird's digestive system. This strange arrangement actually works in favour of both the plant and the bird – both parties benefit.

Climbing ivy

roots

roots

Ivy berries early December

Berry cut open to show 2 seeds

Blackbirds and pigeons, particularly, eat these seeds during the winter.

Bushes

Bushes in gardens are often there for decorative purposes, giving a nice colour throughout the year. They vary in size. They stand alone or are often planted in groups to make the garden more attractive. Others, like Elder and blackberry, thrive in hedges. Some birds, like the Wood Pigeon, nest in big bushes (they like Holly for example) or in big trees, but rarely in hedges. For one thing, a dense hedge leaves no room for a big bird like a pigeon to get in.

Trees

All kinds of trees may grow in a hedge, including big oaks, beech and ash. Some of the smaller trees, like the Mountain Ash and Hawthorn, are sometimes part of a hedge but can also grow into quite tall trees.

In the really big trees, rooks and crows nest near their tops, jays, pigeons and doves in the middle and smaller birds, like Hedge Sparrows, may nest at the ends of lower branches.

Then there are those that nest in holes, but only the woodpeckers actually make holes. A collection of wood chips on the ground below will give it away. Since they usually use them only once, each year there are new holes being excavated and old ones available for other birds. Chief amongst these are Starlings, Nuthatches, Great Tits and Blue Tits, all choosing holes suited to their size.

Do you know where owls nest?

Some, like the Barn Owl, nest (of course) in barns – if convenient ledges near the roof are available. But the Tawny Owl (the owl that hoots – the Barn Owl screeches) likes to nest in holes in trees. However, it is a large bird so it has to find large holes or hollowed-out trees. Little owls, being much smaller, can more easily find holes and hollows.

By the way, did you know that owls eat the whole of their prey, bones, fur and all?

After digesting their meal, they spit out all these tough bits in pellets that can sometimes be found on the ground. They're known as 'owl pellets' and you can tell that an owl has been there even if you never see it. If you are clever enough – and don't mind looking – you can even tell what it's been eating by looking at the contents – bones of small animals like voles and field mice and the hard wing cases of beetles.

Seeds

Do you know how plants multiply?

They do it in several different ways. Most plants produce seeds, but some also produce new plants which grow away from the mother plant, or new bulbs are formed.

For example, irises spread by special thickened stems called 'rhizomes'. These help to form new plants a few centimetres away each year. This is why irises form dense clumps.

Strawberries, including the smaller wild strawberry, spread by 'runners'.

These are rather wiry stems that grow out sideways for about 10cm, and then produce a small tuft of leaves and a small tuft of roots. In this way, a new plant is formed, still connected to the parent plant to help it get settled.

In these sorts of ways plants can gradually spread and form a patch of the same species.

To produce new plants at a distance, however, plants need seeds. First they flower, then, when the flowers have been pollinated and died down, the seeds form.

Wild strawberry with new plants growing from 'runners'

Some of the easiest seeds to see and investigate are those of the Bluebell. When the flowers have died down in late spring, each flower produces a seedpod, which, after some weeks, turns brown and papery and opens at the top.

Seed head growing with petals still attached

Seed head from the side...

... and top

3-sided

Ripe seed head shedding seeds

Each of these cups contains about 12 shiny brown seeds and you can just tip them out into a plastic bag or your hand. If you put them in a small plastic container so that the seeds can be spread out, it is quite easy to count the seeds.

The Bluebell is thus very efficient in multiplying, because the seeds can spread about whilst, in addition, the plant enlarges its clump by splitting off new white bulbs underground, quite deep – about 12cm.

Sometimes seeds are produced in very large numbers, especially if the seeds are small, like the tiny poppy seeds which are produced in their thousands. Big seeds are produced in small numbers. For example, beans or peas are large seeds, with about 10 in a pod. But there is only one hazelnut seed in its shell per flower.

The reason is that big seeds contain lots of stored food for the young plant to use in its early growth, whereas the seedlings from small seeds have to grow leaves very quickly to make their own food. The leaves do this by using sunlight to give them energy.

So seedlings from big seeds have a better chance of survival than from little seeds but the plant can't produce so many of them.

There are an enormous number of different shapes, sizes and colours of seeds – in fact, the seeds of one plant species are usually quite different from those of others.

Have a look at some of them, for example:

The big green acorns from oak trees and the brown conkers from Horse Chestnut trees.

Green acorns

Brown conkers

Winged seeds ('helicopters') from Sycamore and Ash trees.

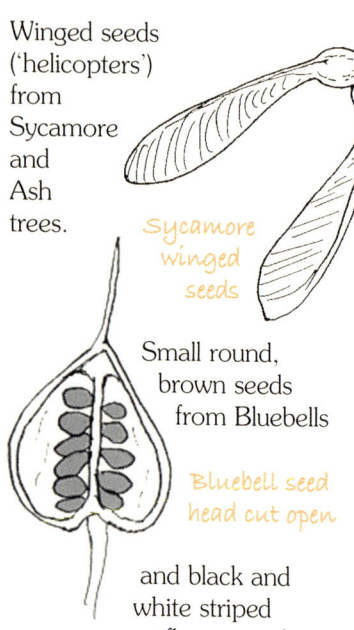

Sycamore winged seeds

Small round, brown seeds from Bluebells

Bluebell seed head cut open

and black and white striped sunflower seeds.

Sunflower seeds

Some seeds are formed in the middle of fruits, such as:

Apple
Cherry
Pear
Rose hips
Hawthorn berries

How do you think seeds are spread?

After all, it wouldn't be much good if all the seeds just dropped around the parent plant? For instance, it would not be good for all the acorns of a particular oak tree to try to grow in the shade of their big parent.

The best chance for a seed is to be away from its parent, so that it doesn't compete for light and water.

How do you think this happens?

Fruits are often eaten by birds and other animals, which carry them away and either leave the seeds (e.g. cherry stones) or eat them, as birds do with mistletoe berries, and the seeds are then found in their droppings. Squirrels will hide nuts in the ground as storage for the winter.

Many seeds have special ways of being blown about in the wind.

Dandelion shedding seeds

Doubtless you have seen dandelion seeds with their little parachutes.

Similarly, the seeds of willow trees and willow herb are attached to soft, cotton-like fluff and are therefore carried easily by the wind.

Willow seed with fluff

The huge willow trees produce

these, which look like a lot of down floating about in the air. The seeds are tiny (0.1mm). In fact, the drawing shows details you could only see under a microscope.

Lots of trees have winged seeds, like the sycamore, ash tree or lime tree, which helps them to be blown away from the mother tree. The seedpods of lime trees have a single wing attached to them.

Lime tree seedpods with wing

Single seedpod with 4 to 5 ridges

Seedpod cut open

Each pod has one seed, which is dark brown and slightly pointed, and is covered by a hard coat. When you cut open the seed you will find a creamy plant embryo.

Seed

4mm

Inside of seed showing plant embryo

Poppy seed head

Small holes

When the seed heads of poppies dry and you shake them, you can hear the seeds rattle inside. Normally the wind will sway them, spraying seeds about which can escape from small holes.

Other seeds don't need the wind but rely on the plant flinging them about!

You can see this best in Cranesbill or Stork's Bill. The flowers produce a spike with arms pointing downwards.

Cranesbill ready to release seeds

Seed heads

Enlarged seed head before...

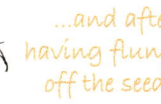

...and after having flung off the seeds

At the end of each arm is a big seed. When the whole seed head becomes dry, these arms suddenly spring outwards, flinging the seed some distance away.

Some seeds are spread by sticking to things, like the seeds of Goosegrass do. The hairs on the seed head have curved ends so they hook on to passing animals and carry the seeds to another place. This is how the plant spreads its seeds from where it originally grew.

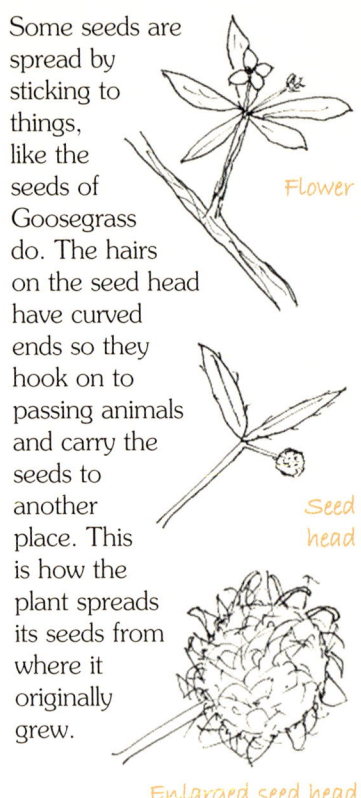

Flower

Seed head

Enlarged seed head

Enlarged hooks on seed head

Daffodils are good examples to show how seeds are formed. They finish flowering (depending on whether it's an early or late spring) in April/May. As the bright yellow or orange petals shrivel, the base of the flower swells up.

Daffodil and development of seeds

Flower

Swelling of base

Seedpod closed

Seedpod opened to show seeds

Inside you will find a central column with rows of small white seeds growing all round it.

No-one will mind you pulling off the heads of daffodils after they have flowered, in fact, gardeners often do this, partly for the sake of tidiness and partly so that the plant puts all its energy into growing a big bulb (underground) for next year and not wasting it on seeds. So you can pick as many as you want. If you do this every few days, you can see how the seeds grow, week by week.

The only thing you need to be careful about is how you open the dark green seedpod, which is quite tough. If you use a sharp knife, be careful not to cut yourself.

How many seeds are in a daffodil seedpod?

When the pods are opened, you could try counting the seeds. There are usually quite a lot – 60 or 70.

Snowdrops have pods rather like daffodils but much smaller

Snowdrop seed head

Seed head sliced open

When they are opened up, the way the little white seeds are arranged is quite similar to those of the daffodil.

When seeds germinate and burst into life, the first leaves to appear are not always like those that the plant grows afterwards.

The sycamore seedling is a very good example of this.

Sycamore seedling

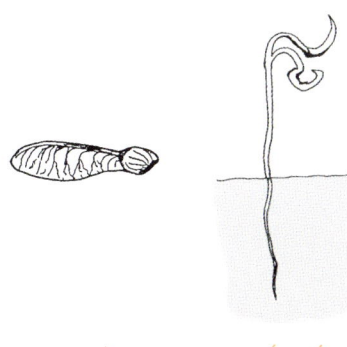
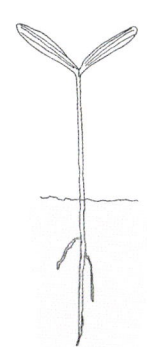

Seed *Germination* *Seedling with the first leaves* *Seedling with first and second pair of leaves*

55

What's under logs and stones?

Clearly only small animals can possibly be under logs and stones, although it is surprising how some beetles, and especially earthworms, manage to make tunnels in the moist earth beneath.

What may you expect to find if you lift up a flat stone or log?

Earthworms are quite common, and **black ants** often choose to make their nests underneath flat stones. Most of the nest, of course, is underground. You can also find many different **beetles** which just squeeze between the stone and the soil, but probably these and other small animals, like **slugs**, are more common under logs where they find more space.

Here you may find many other small creatures like **millipedes**, **centipedes** and **woodlice**, as well as **spiders** and **mites**.

What do all these animals feed on?

Where do they lay their eggs? Do they get on with each other?

Earthworms, slugs and woodlice will feed on rotting wood and benefit from the protection of logs or stones as well as the moisture. None of them want to risk being dried up by the sun or wind.

Slugs often lay their round, pearly-white eggs on the underside of a log. The eggs may be more than 1mm across. You can be sure that the only **snails** that can squeeze under logs are the small flat ones. These lay much smaller eggs.

Woodlice find food under the logs in the form of rotting wood and fungus growing on it.

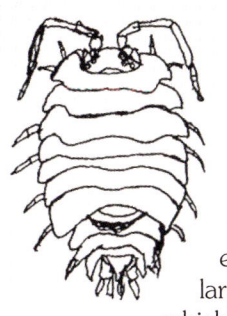
Woodlouse

Beetle Larvae

Devil's Coach Horse larva

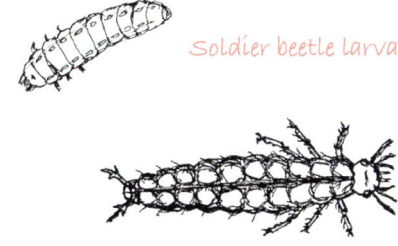
Soldier beetle larva

Violet Ground Beetle larva

There is one kind of spider with especially large jaws, which feeds on woodlice, the **Woodlouse spider**. It can also be found under logs during the day, but they hunt during the night.

Millipedes, too, feed on rotting vegetation.

Millipede

Even though they have many legs, they move very slowly and need a hard outer coat to be protected against predators, as do beetles and woodlice. Centipedes, however, are hunters and move fast to catch other small animals.

Slugs and their eggs are soft and therefore easy prey to predators. Of course, you may also find a great variety of other eggs and grub-like small creatures, mostly the larvae of beetles which are soft and may get eaten.

Earwigs are also found under logs and in crevices and like to rest where both upper and lower parts of their body are in touch with the surfaces they lie between. They feed on small creatures, both alive and dead, as well as decaying plant material, like leaves. They lay their eggs in the soil and look after them by licking them clean and defending them from predators.

Most of the beetles are hunters, like the Ground Beetle, and often attack slugs; so do centipedes.

Another beetle is the extraordinary Devil's Coach Horse. It defends itself by raising its tail over its back and squirting a smelly liquid in the face of an attacker. It is quite big, about 2.5 cm long, and shiny black. It lives under logs

Devil's Coach Horse

and leaves, and hunts worms, spiders and smaller beetles, mainly at night, but is harmless to humans.

Spiders are also hunters but do not seem to eat slugs. Why is this? Perhaps the spiders dislike the slime, or their jaws are not strong enough to bite into slugs. Even birds take quite a lot of effort to eat a slug, constantly wiping the slime from their beaks.

A lot of the predators feed on mites. These are very small, around 1mm long, and, like spiders, have eight legs. They are all rather round and the most noticeable ones are bright red.

Mite

five at actual size

Another animal that looks rather like a spider and also has eight legs is the **Harvestman** – but there is one big difference.

Have you noticed that the bodies of spiders are divided into two parts?

There is the front bit, which is a sort of combined head and chest, and the hind part, which is called the abdomen. Now, the harvestman has no such division, it just has one rather rounded body – so it has no waist as such. It stands quite high on its legs and is a hunter, mostly active at night, feeding on worms, snails and small insects. They are found throughout the garden, often under logs and loose vegetation, but you will also find them on walls.

Harvestman from above...

...and from the side

There is another rather odd difference. If a spider loses a leg it can grow another one, so you rarely find a spider that has less than eight legs. Harvestman can't do this and quite often shed a leg if they are roughly handled, so you may often find a Harvestman with fewer than eight legs.

Toads like to eat slugs; they manage to squeeze under logs which provide big enough spaces. With time, the wood rots away underneath and becomes soft, so bigger spaces develop.

Newts, too, especially young ones (in their first year after leaving the pond), hide and feed under logs.

What's in the long grass?

There's not much to be found in short grass, like the lawn.

The lawnmower is surely not very popular amongst the insects and other small creatures that inhabit our lawns. Lots of them live under the grass, in the soil; therefore you don't see much of them.

You see worm 'casts', the soil that **earthworms** have eaten and passed right through their bodies to form 'strings' of soil in little heaps. But these get squashed by the mower, as do any small anthills that the small yellow lawn ants make.

If the lawn contains clover or daisies in flower, bees will be attracted to them, to collect nectar and pollen. But the bees are only visiting, as they don't live here but in their hive.

Long grass is different.

Wood mouse

The biggest animals living in long grass are **wood mice**, **voles** and **shrews**. Wood mice and voles are about the same size, but shrews are smaller.

Field vole

They are all brownish and furry mammals, with bright, beady, dark eyes and whiskers on their noses.

You can tell the difference if they stay still long enough for you to see them clearly because:

Shrew

Wood mice have

very pointed noses,
large ears
and long tails.

Voles have

blunt, rounded noses,
small ears
and short tails.

Shrews have

long snouts,
very small ears
and medium-sized tails.

Wood mice jump away, but voles and shrews run down tunnels that they make through the grass.

How animals grow

There are two sorts of insects – those that have stages like caterpillars (also called larvae) and pupae as in butterflies and those that just gradually get bigger as with grasshoppers.

How do they do this?

You may think, what's the problem? This is how we grow, isn't it?

Our skeleton, with all our bones, is on the inside of our body, so we get bigger as long as it grows.

Their nests were described earlier as were those of the **bumblebees** that make very similar nests at the bottom of long grass.

All sorts of **beetles** can be found running about on the ground in long grass, but the insects that you may see on the grass itself are the grasshoppers.

Insects don't have bones to hold them up. They have a hard covering on the outside and this doesn't stretch. Examples are the hard wing cases of beetles, like ladybirds. When you examine them, you can see that they are stiff and therefore don't get bigger.

So how do grasshoppers manage?

The answer is that they moult.

You may have heard of dogs and cats moulting? It simply means shedding the outer hairs. Foxes do it, too, and in

60

Grasshoppers eat the grass and, when disturbed, jump quite long distances – up to a metre – using their huge hind legs.

Garden Grasshopper

However, lots of insects don't grow like this!

For example butterflies: their young are caterpillars and they look nothing like the adult butterflies that they will become.

They lay eggs on the grass and when these hatch, out come miniature grasshoppers – very small copies of the parents.

Garden Snail shell

Shell of small flat snail

the autumn you may see a fox that looks 'moth-eaten', with patches of hair missing.

In grasshoppers, and insects like them, it means shedding the whole of the hard outer skin. A new soft skin has grown underneath and, before it hardens, the insect swells up, so that when the new skin does harden, it is a larger size.

Crabs that you see on the seashore have the same growth problem because of their very hard shells, and they have the same solution: they also moult. You don't see them doing this, because they hide away whilst they only have soft skins and are not protected by their hard shells.

So why don't snails do the same?

Have a look at a snail shell and you'll see that they have a spiral shape, starting with a little circle at the top and spiralling round and round and getting bigger.

So the snail can add more shell at the big end, where the snail body comes out, and thus make room for it as it grows.

You can see that the main difference between the shell of a snail and that of a crab is that the snail's shell is not really part of the body of the animal; it is a home that it makes to live in. The body of the snail can gradually get bigger and it just builds a bigger house for it.

A banded snail

The kind of snails that you often find in long grass are smaller than the Common Garden Snail and instead of being coloured brown (with black bits) they have 'bands' of black and yellow or brown and yellow circling round the shell; hence their name: **banded snails**. The shells are rather fragile and easily damaged.

Shrews feed on them and in some places you can find a collection of their empty shells. You may also find them a metre or more up bushes and tall plants.

You will also find **slugs** in long grass. These are really snails that no longer have shells.

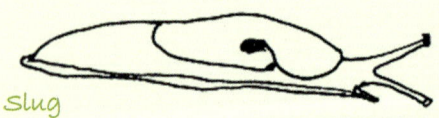

Slug

Lots of people dislike slugs:

What do you think about slugs?

They can't help being slimy – this is how they move about. They slide over the slime that they have made. Gardeners don't like them because of the damage they do to their favourite plants. Not all slugs eat growing plants; some eat dead leaves and do no harm at all.

Other creatures that live in long grass are **spiders**. Actually, different kinds of spider are found everywhere and there are enormous numbers of them.

Some are quite small and can be found on flowers, for example, often the same colour as the flower so their prey does not easily detect them. Others spin webs, made of silk, which they use to trap insects for their food.

Some of these webs are large (up to 20cm across) and easy to see. They are very beautifully made and it is hard to see how the spiders manage to attach them across quite large gaps.

Spider in its web

Others are very difficult to see. For instance, very fine webs are made on the short grass of lawns but you can only see them when heavy dew covers them with tiny drops of water or the sunlight glints off them.

In long grass there are two sorts of spider: ones that spin webs between the blades of grass and others that live on the soil in which the grass grows.

In the autumn, you can see lots of '**Daddy Long-legs**' or crane flies, sometimes in swarms.

What do you think these insects are doing in the long grass?

They are there to lay their shiny, black eggs in the damp soil under the grass: each female can lay up to 500 eggs! These eggs hatch to become tough, leathery, legless grubs, 3-4cm long, called 'leatherjackets'.

They do a lot of damage by eating grass roots, so are considered a pest by farmers. They live in the soil before turning into new crane flies the following May.

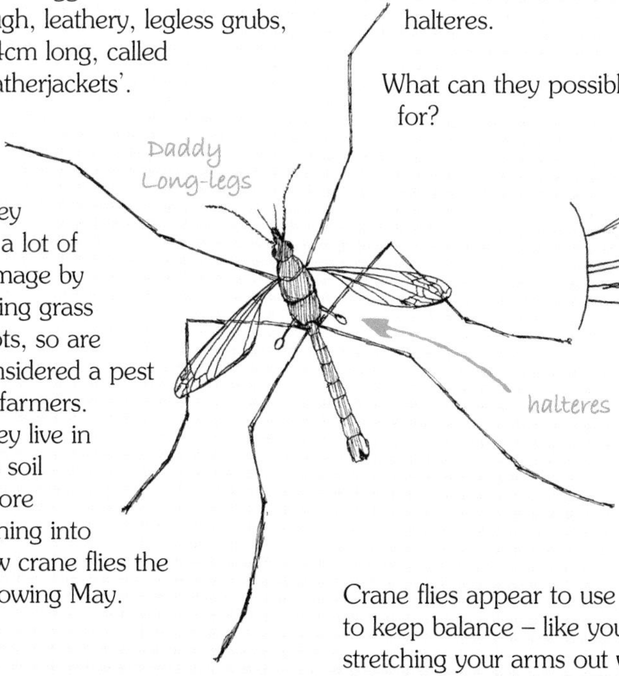

They are quite big insects and have the usual six legs but they only have one pair of wings. Bees, wasps and butterflies, you remember, have two pairs of wings, often with the fore and hind wings joined together by hooks.

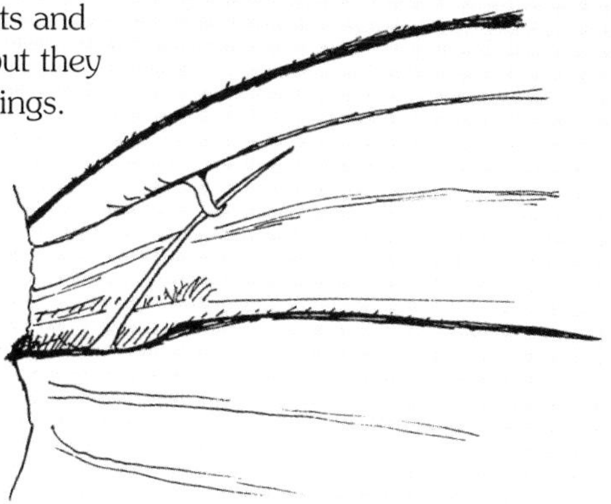

Instead of hind wings, crane flies have a pair of little knobs called halteres.

What can they possibly be for?

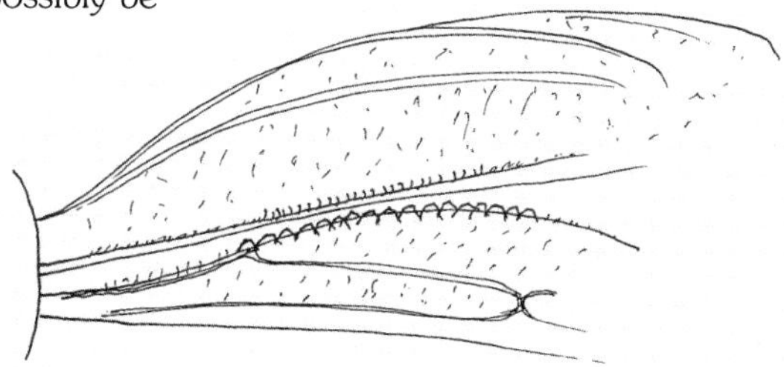

Crane flies appear to use them to keep balance – like you stretching your arms out when you walk along a log or on a wall. Actually, lots of flies, including the housefly, have them, but they are very difficult to see.

Daddy Long-legs

halteres

Joining of front and hind wings of a butterfly by a clasp

Joining of front and hind wings of a wasp by small hooks

63

Hunters

Do you think there are more hunters than animals that are hunted?

Suppose that foxes only ate rabbits (they don't of course, but just suppose), there couldn't be as many foxes as rabbits, could there? Otherwise, in one week, all the rabbits would be eaten and the foxes would have nothing to live on.

Clearly, the fox is bigger than the rabbit, so it's going to eat several in a year. Thus there must be more rabbits than foxes.

And the rabbits have to keep on breeding to produce lots of new rabbits to replace those eaten. But this would not be enough if the foxes were multiplying at the same rate.

Fortunately, the fox only produces one litter a year, of 4-5 cubs, whilst the rabbit breeds up to seven times a year, usually with a litter of five. In fact, in the spring the rabbit can produce one litter each month and can start breeding at an early age. If they're born in the early spring, they can breed that same year.

This is generally how it works: the predators (those that eat other animals) multiply more slowly than their prey (those that get eaten).

Fox hunting earthworms

This is just as well, when you think that an owl may catch 20 voles and a fox may eat 100 earthworms in one night.

Ladybirds can eat 20 or so greenfly each day and each spider eats at least 20 insects in a year, probably more. Almost everything that lives, even the predator, has something that eats it.

Only the biggest and fiercest are not attacked. Even then, other animals may steal their eggs or eat their young, or attack them when they are old, injured or diseased.

It is true that foxes don't just live on rabbits; they also eat beetles, earthworms, wood mice and voles, for example.

But it is also true that it is not only foxes that eat rabbits since they are also eaten by owls, stoats and weasels.

So the hunters usually live on a number of different sorts of prey and this helps them to find food at all times of the year. For example, most earthworms are found on the surface of the ground (especially the lawn) on warm, moist nights and there are more rabbits about in the spring.

Of course, the small hunters are also hunted!

How do the hunters catch their prey?

Obviously, in lots of different ways, even within one group of animals. Some spiders spin sticky silken webs to catch flies; but others – the jumping spiders – just leap on the insects they want to eat. One of these is the Zebra spider, which lives on the outside walls of houses and gets its name from its black and white stripes.

Zebra spider

Some animals, such as frogs, just lie in wait (like a cat watching a mouse-hole), others rush about searching for food (centipedes do this), whilst others find out where the prey is hiding or dig it out (woodpeckers dig out grubs under tree bark and thrushes find snails hidden behind logs or big stones).

If you were hunting, what would you do?

You might also lie in wait but, unless you were on a horse, you probably wouldn't chase after anything, unless it was much slower than you (like a frog). But you would use your eyes, wouldn't you? You wouldn't feel for things or track them by smell, and you certainly wouldn't do it by taste!

But different animals use all these senses.

Foxes use their sense of *smell*.

Owls *hear* the scuttling of mice, even in complete darkness.

Snakes *taste* the air – that's what their forked tongue is doing – and *feel* tiny vibrations made by prey.

Some fish and some ducks *feel* their prey in muddy water or even in the mud itself.

Most birds use *sight* and many of them can *see* tiny creatures a long way off.

If you watch a Robin, you will notice that it chooses a handy perch, such as your garden fork or wheelbarrow, and spots a worm or an insect that you can't see, then swoops down and gobbles it up.

Most animals seem to be rather like us: one of our senses (in our case, sight) is much better than the others.

Some animals have extra senses that we do not seem to use.

Snakes, for example, can sense *heat* and follow the source of it, such as a mouse. We can certainly feel heat but we couldn't easily locate something in that way, unless it was very hot.

Bats have their own ways of 'seeing' things. They send out very high frequency sounds and can tell where things are and how far away they are by listening to the sounds bouncing back at them.

Have you ever heard an echo? You shout out and your voice comes back to you soon afterwards.

Well, bats are doing the same thing but incredibly fast. The speed of their reactions is what strikes us.

How do you think dragonflies catch the insects they feed on?

They can see very well with their enormous eyes.

Head and eyes of a dragonfly (greatly enlarged)

Compound eye

Detail of the compound eye showing six-sided units

And they can twist and turn in the air in an amazing way – they can even fly backwards!

Blue Tit collecting insects

It's much the same with birds, although none of our birds can fly backwards!

You and I can't even see what they're catching, it all happens so quickly.

Birds can also hear very well: you may see blackbirds on the lawn with their heads cocked on one side, listening to worms wriggling below the surface.

However, lots of animals can't see colours as we do. When you think how useful we find colour in seeing birds, it is surprising that animals, which depend on their sight to find food, often do not have this ability.

But many animals, such as foxes and owls, see much better at night than we do. Both creatures also hear much better than we do. To help them in this, foxes have very large ears that they can move, each one separately. This helps them to tell where the sound is coming from.

Barn owl swooping on prey

Big ears make a lot of sense, if you depend on hearing. You can test that by cupping your ears with your hands. So why do barn owls have such small ears that you can't even see them?

All these senses – seeing, hearing, smelling, feeling and tasting – are used by the hunters to find their prey. They then have to catch them and kill them.

Catching may involve speed, as with birds that move much faster than the creatures they eat, or stealth (creeping up on them quietly and unseen). But, in many cases, it is only a matter of finding them.

Song Thrush breaking open a snail shell

Snail

Anvil

Fragments of broken shells

Song thrushes only have to find a snail, not catch it. Therefore slow-moving animals often have hard coats. The thrushes have to break the snail's shell which they do by banging it on a stone.

They often use special stones or brick paths for this, where you can find collections of broken shells.

When the prey is caught, it has to be killed to prevent it escaping again or it may just be eaten. Therefore, hunters are often armed with sharp teeth or claws.

The fox has teeth for biting and for chewing. Birds have no teeth, but flesh-eating birds, such as owls, kestrels and sparrow-hawks, have sharply curved beaks, whilst insect-eaters have pointed beaks, and those eating seeds have short strong beaks, like the goldfinch. You can often tell what a bird eats by looking at the shape of its beak.

Some animals just swallow their prey. A newt or a frog simply swallows an insect whole and a snake, which cannot chew anything, just swallows the whole animal – mouse or frog – even if it is quite big. Fish do the same.

The snake's jaws are specially designed to separate in order

Shapes of bird beaks

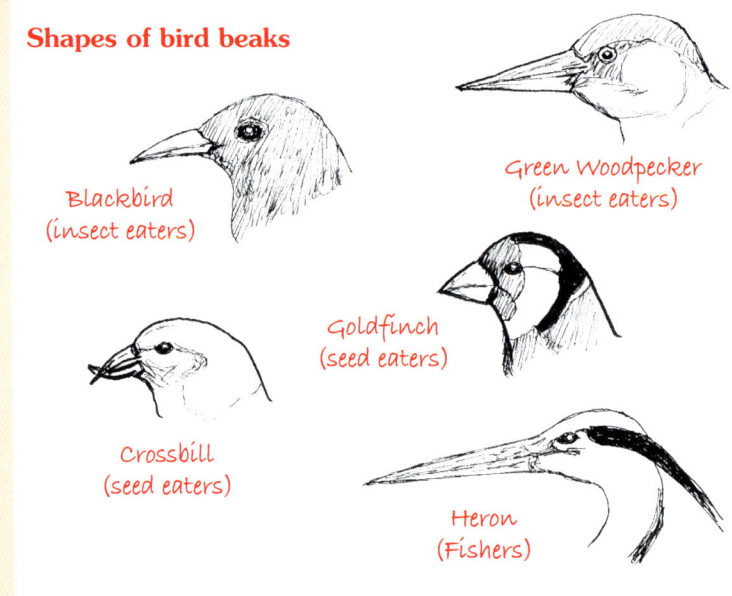

Blackbird (insect eaters)

Green Woodpecker (insect eaters)

Crossbill (seed eaters)

Goldfinch (seed eaters)

Heron (Fishers)

to widen the mouth for swallowing big prey. This does not seem very nice for the prey but they rapidly suffocate when they are swallowed.

Spiders catch insects in their sticky webs and often wrap them up in silk and keep them for later.

Some bigger animals also store food. Foxes bury dead food and dig it up again later. Shrews and moles may store live earthworms after they have bitten them so they can't move away.

Animals that have to feed their young, like foxes and birds, have to be able to carry the food to them. Foxes use their jaws whilst birds use their beaks or feet.

Snakes don't feed their young, which is just as well, since they seem unable to carry anything!

You might think that hunters would not be brightly coloured, because the prey could see them coming. But that doesn't apply to birds. Why is this?

Well, I suppose one answer is that they are so much faster than the insects (or even mice and rabbits, in the case of bigger birds) that they feed on.

For the same reason, dragonflies are often brightly coloured, but they are very fast, whether they are chasing or being chased.

It would be no good, of course, if it was too difficult to catch prey – the hunters would go hungry and die out – or too easy, for then all the prey would get eaten up and there would be none left to produce the next generation.

So there is a rough balance between numbers of hunters and numbers of hunted but it does not stay like that all the time. In some years there are more prey, then the next year the number of hunters would increase. And so on.

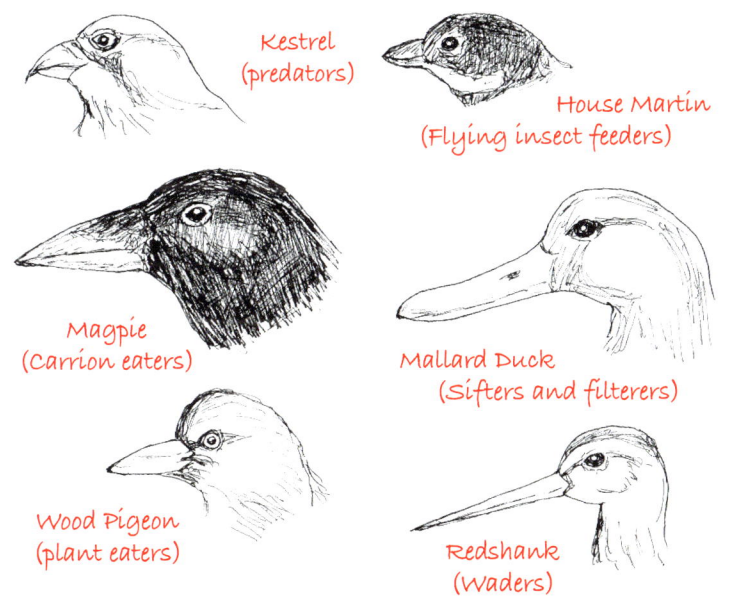

Kestrel (predators)

House Martin (Flying insect feeders)

Magpie (Carrion eaters)

Mallard Duck (Sifters and filterers)

Wood Pigeon (plant eaters)

Redshank (Waders)

The Hunted

Are there any animals in your garden that are not hunted by other animals, I wonder?

Why might they be safe?

Perhaps because they're big or fierce.

Even the biggest are small when they're young and they all become old and frail eventually.

So it may be that no animal is quite safe, but some are less safe than others.

I can immediately think of
- **foxes hunting rabbits and mice**
- **owls hunting voles**
- **bats hunting moths**
- **spiders hunting flies**
- **ladybirds hunting greenfly**

and I expect you can think of lots of others.

Since not all the animals that are hunted get killed and eaten, how do they survive?

How about hiding?

Many creatures do this. Woodlice and slugs hide under logs or the bark of trees.

Caterpillars hide amongst the leaves of the plant they are feeding on. Since they cannot move very far or very fast, they hide where they feed, using colour to help them look like part of the plant.

Looking like the background also helps some butterflies to hide. Have you noticed that even very brightly coloured butterflies seem to disappear when they come to rest?

A Painted Lady resting

This is because they close their wings above them so that you can't see the bright colours: the undersides of the wings – which you can see – are quite dull.

Mice and voles hide amongst long grass or in holes in the ground. So do rabbits, but they have to come out to feed.

Of course, it is not only prey animals that need to avoid being seen; the hunters may also need to remain hidden so that their prey are not frightened off.

Slow-moving animals also have other ways of protecting themselves. For example, they may taste horrible or even be poisonous!

Toads are not able to jump like frogs do, they can only crawl along. So they taste horrible and are actually poisonous; animals that try to eat them usually give up and put them down again.

Ladybirds are predators, feeding on greenfly, but they would also make a nice meal for birds and ants, except that they produce an unpleasant liquid from the joints of their legs. They advertise the fact that they are harmful by their bright colouring.

Wasps are brightly coloured for the same reason: to give out the message, "Don't attack me, I'm dangerous," (in their case because of their unpleasant sting).

Some animals are protected by their shells (e.g. snails), by being slimy (e.g. slugs), by irritating hairs (e.g. Woolly Bear caterpillars) or by hard coats (e.g. beetles and millipedes).

Hedgehogs are especially well protected, not only by their sharp stiff spines, which they can erect, but also because they can roll into a ball, protecting their soft underside.

Others avoid capture by running, jumping or flying away.

Can you think of examples of these?

Running: Rabbits, mice?
Jumping: Frogs, grasshoppers?
Flying: Houseflies, butterflies?

Have you ever tried to catch a fly? For sure, they are very quick.

Butterflies are very interesting, because they are often brightly coloured, quite big enough to be easily seen and many species don't fly very fast (some species like the Red Admiral and Comma are difficult to follow by eye – let alone catch them!). So why don't birds catch them easily?

I think it is because they 'flutter' rather than flying in a straight line. One effect of this is that you can't tell where they are going to be next. It is rather like catching a falling leaf in the autumn. Have you ever tried to catch one? It doesn't fall straight down – it zigzags all over the place. Even on a windless day it is very hard to do so, as you doubtless know.

Similarly, you cannot catch a frog or a grasshopper by working out where it's going to land or by catching it in flight. You have to catch it just before it jumps – but this is quite difficult.

Have you noticed what big, powerful legs these jumpers have?

As they are not very heavy they can jump very far and also don't appear to hurt themselves when they land. Other small animals, like mice, can drop to the ground from quite a height without getting hurt.

In ponds, small animals, such as freshwater shrimps and water lice, hide in the mud at the bottom, but any movement attracts fish or newts which are likely to gobble them up.

Caddis fly larvae live in the water and have an interesting way of protecting themselves – they build a tube-like case out of leaves, small stones, bits of waterweed or empty snail shells.

Legs of a frog — hind leg, front leg

Caddis fly larva outside its case — Hooks

They hold on to the inside of the case by hooks at their tail-end and poke out their hard heads and legs at the front to pull the tube along.

As they grow bigger, they add on more material at the front or simply move out and build a bigger case.

Cases of caddis fly larvae

Another way of avoiding being eaten is to bury yourself, in soil, deep inside a plant or a log.

The larvae of crane flies live entirely in the soil, for a whole year, and are protected from many predators – except the mole.

The mole makes tunnels under the ground and pushes up the soil it has dug out to form molehills. It travels up and down these tunnels catching grubs and especially earthworms that have fallen in.

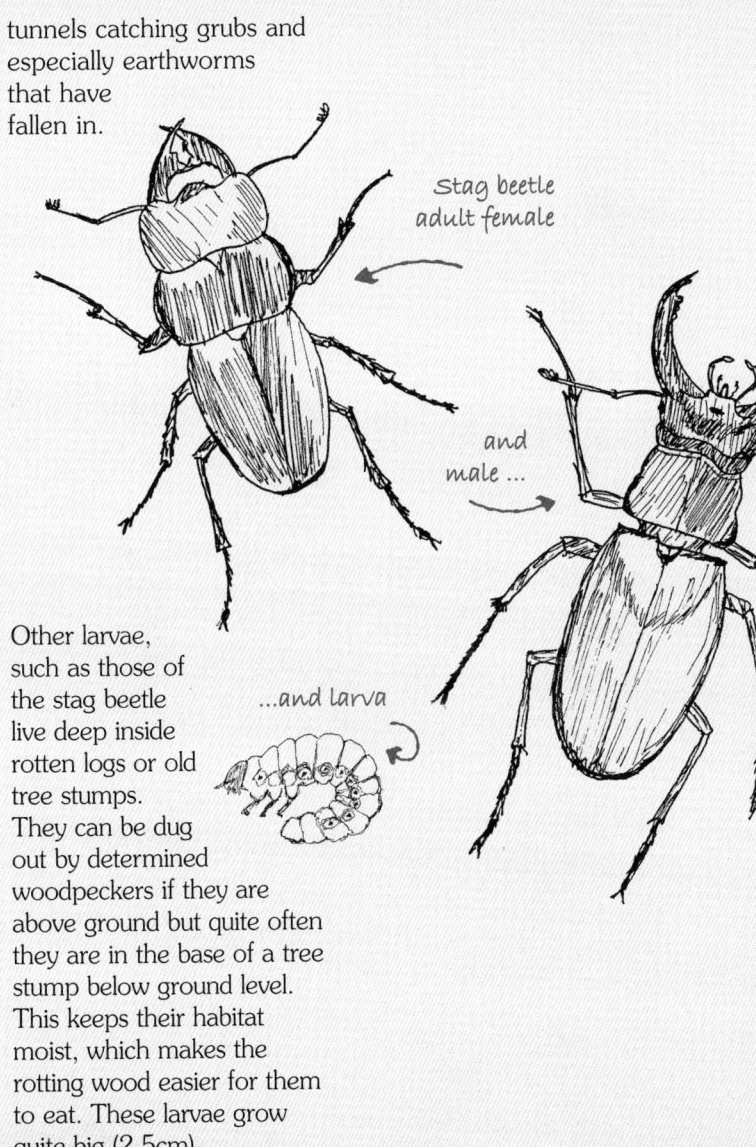

Stag beetle adult female

and male ...

...and larva

Other larvae, such as those of the stag beetle live deep inside rotten logs or old tree stumps. They can be dug out by determined woodpeckers if they are above ground but quite often they are in the base of a tree stump below ground level. This keeps their habitat moist, which makes the rotting wood easier for them to eat. These larvae grow quite big (2.5cm).

A lot of animals only come out at night or at dawn and dusk, when the light is dim. Why is that?

Basically so they can't be seen. But they must be able to see; so why can't their predators see them?

They use other senses than sight.

For example, rabbits come out at night, but so do their predators foxes and owls. Of course, these can hear very well, and don't just depend on sight. Foxes also have an excellent sense of smell and often detect mice and other small creatures in this way.

Bats mostly fly at dusk and dawn to hunt and feed on insects, especially moths. They detect the flying moths by sending out very high squeaks and clicks and listening for their echoes.

What's in the Pond?

Many ponds have fish of course.

Goldfish are the most common because they can easily be seen, due to their size and bright colours – yellow, orange, red and even white.

What do you think fish normally live on?

In the wild and in natural garden ponds, they feed on small creatures that also live in the water. The most common are freshwater shrimps and water lice, but there are also the larvae of water beetles, dragonflies and mayflies.

Small fish eat much smaller creatures, especially water fleas. These are not really fleas, but, like true fleas, they are flattened from side to side and move in a jerky fashion. Very common is also the small pond animal called Cyclops.

Water flea

Cyclops

In a fish tank (aquarium) or small pond, usually more fish are kept than

Freshwater shrimp

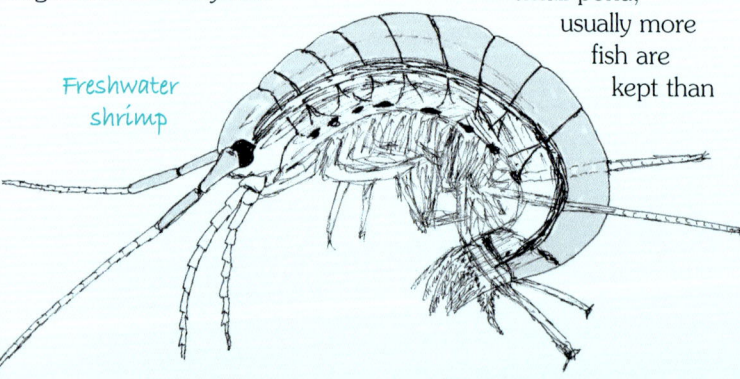

can be supplied with natural food. So they have to be fed, often with ant pupae sold as ants' eggs.

In fact, a pond doesn't need fish. Without them there is actually much more life in form of tiny creatures and the animals that live on them.

The easiest to see are those that live on the surface and those that swim up to the surface every now and again.

Why do they do that?

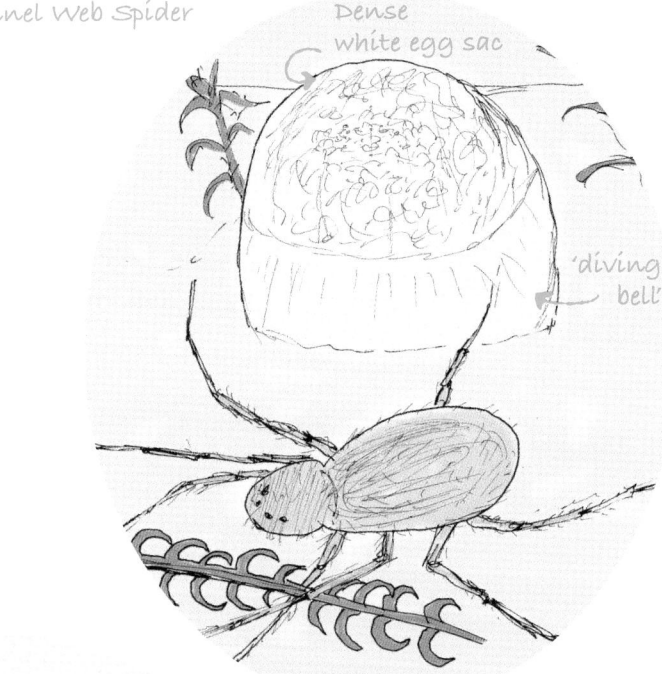

Funnel Web Spider

Dense white egg sac

'diving bell'

Great Diving Beetle taking on air

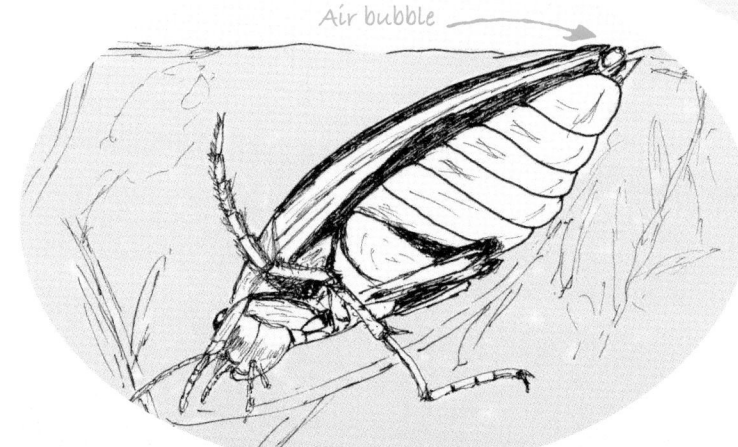

Air bubble

It is to breathe air. If you watch a water beetle carefully, when it comes up to the surface it traps a bubble of air under its wing cases or in hairs at its tail.

Some water spiders actually build a tent-like web amongst the weeds and carry bubbles of air down in order to breathe.

Water boatman can easily be seen in ponds. They're quite large (about 12mm long) and swim on their backs. That's why they're also called 'backswimmers'. Their third pair of legs (the hind one) is big and strong and is used like a pair of oars to pull themselves along.

Compound eyes

Swimming leg

Water boatman - upperside

How come that some insects get trapped in the water and others, like the pond skater, can move freely on it, with no difficulty?

It obviously can't be the weight, as the pond skater is clearly heavier than its prey, the trapped insects.

Why on earth do they swim upside down?

The answer is that they feed on insects trapped on the surface, so when they come up from below, they are facing their food, which they stab with their pointed 'beaks'.

Similarly, pond skaters feed on trapped insects using their beaks but do it from above or alongside them.

Pond skater with side view of head showing 'beak'

antennae

beak

There are several reasons why the pond skater can skate. Firstly it spreads its weight by having long legs and its only points of contact with the water are its feet.

Insect prey on water surface

Enlarged foot of Pond skater

unwettable hairs

Water boatman - upside down hanging by its shorter legs from the water surface before stabbing its prey.

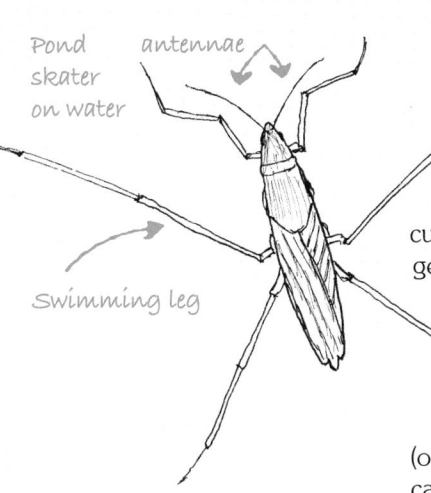

Pond skater on water
antennae
Swimming leg

Try floating a dead leaf on the water. It doesn't sink. That is because, even if it is quite a heavy leaf, the weight is spread over quite a lot of water surface.

But why don't the pond skater's feet pierce the water?

The water has a film on its surface, a special layer of water, almost as though it had a very thin layer of plastic on it. Insects that fall into the water break this film and get wet, especially their wings, and are trapped.

Why then don't the feet of the pond skater get wet?

It is because they end in curved, unwettable hairs that gently rest on the surface film, making small dips in it. You can see these around each foot and if the sunlight shines on them (or light from a torch), they cast circular shadows on the bottom of the pond.

All insects are 'cold-blooded'. Thus they don't keep themselves warm as we do. Even when we are sitting still, our body manages to keep warm and gets even warmer when we exercise our muscles.

Most insects don't work like that, although some species can warm up their flight muscles by vibrating the wings. They depend upon their surroundings, like the sunshine, to warm them.

Also frogs, toads, newts, snails, slugs, woodlice and centipedes are cold-blooded, and they hide away in the winter.

So why don't water boatman and other small animals in the pond have to do the same?

It's because water in ponds rarely freezes (depending on the severity of the winter and the depth of the pond), except at the surface where it forms ice. Underneath this ice, the water remains liquid and thus can support the animals and plants living in it. Mind you, all the small animals slow down; they only get really active when the environment warms up.

Some animals only live in the water for part of the year. Frogs and toads visit the pond solely to mate and to lay their eggs (spawn). Newts do the same but stay for several months because they lay eggs one at a time over a period of several weeks, whereas frogs and toads lay all their eggs at once.

What goes on in the pond therefore varies from one time of the year to another.

Lots of insects also come to mate and lay their eggs, including dragonflies, damselflies, mosquitoes, midges and mayflies. Mostly they just dip their tails in the water or lay their eggs on the surface. The only eggs that are easy to see are the rafts of eggs produced by mosquitoes.

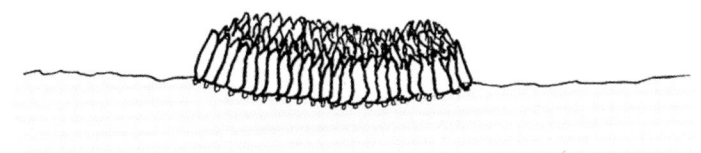

Raft of mosquito eggs floating on water

Midges also lay their eggs in the water but they are too small to see. What you can see, if you look very carefully, are the larvae of phantom midges

Side view and...

...view from above of a phantom midge

They are about 8mm long, almost transparent, with a black dot at each end.

They lie horizontally (that is parallel with the water surface) and most of the time stay quite still. When they do move, it's by a quick jerk and they suddenly appear a few centimetres away from where they were.

Also, they lie several centimetres from the bottom but not on the surface, so you have to search for them. Once you have seen them, you will find it much easier to spot them again.

Birds visit the pond to drink and, more often, to bathe. Blackbirds and starlings, particularly, seem to enjoy this but they need a shallow place or a flat stone to stand on.

In very large ponds, ducks and moorhens may nest. Mallard, our commonest duck, nest on islands or on the bank. They don't make much of a nest, mostly a hollow amongst dead leaves, and their eggs (as many as ten) are pale coloured and large: so, when they leave the nest to get food, they cover them up with leaves.

Moorhens build their nests on or very close to the water, in clumps of rushes or water iris or fixed on to floating branches. Very often they bend the rushes or iris leaves over the nest to form a thin roof, mostly to prevent the eggs being seen by predators from above.

Both duck and moorhen eggs are stolen by grey squirrels, foxes (if they can reach them) and large birds (e.g. crows, magpies). Very often, if their eggs are stolen, they will lay another clutch.

The Garden at night

What is happening in your garden at night?

Most of the birds find a safe place to roost (sleep) and they stay very quiet. Did you know that they have a special way of perching, with the feet locked in position so that they cannot fall off?

Not all birds sleep at night, however. Can you think of some that are active at night and not in the daytime?

What about owls?

You are more likely to hear than to see them – the screech of the Barn Owls and the hoots of the Tawny Owls.

Clearly, there would be no point in owls hunting at night if there were nothing to hunt!

So it's not surprising that mice, voles and rabbits come out at night, more especially at dawn and dusk, than in daylight. Partly for this reason so do foxes.

It surprises many people that, at certain times of the year, foxes eat lots of earthworms. They do this at night when the worms come out onto the surface of the lawn, for example. Earthworms like a warm, moist night, which stops them from drying out, and with lots of dead leaves to pull down into their burrows.

Of course, it's very hard to see any of these animals by going out at night. Rabbits, foxes and badgers will often trigger security lights and don't seem to be bothered by this at all.

If you ever thought that nothing was happening at night, go out early in the morning when there is a covering of snow on the ground. You will see an astonishing number of tracks and will be able to tell who made them.

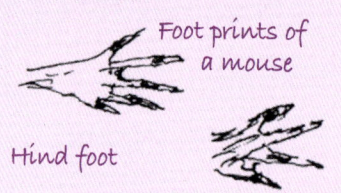

Foot prints of a mouse

Hind foot

Front foot

Foot prints of a shrew

Hind foot
Front foot

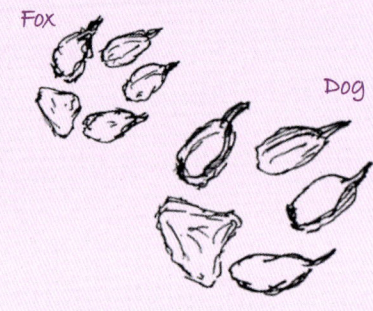

Fox

Dog

Most of the bird tracks you see will have been made in daylight, very early in the morning, but the other animals will be found to have criss-crossed the garden several times.

In the summer, tracks will only be seen where there is wet mud.

On warm summer nights you may see lots of snails, slugs, woodlice and occasionally a toad. I regularly see one in a very peculiar place. It is sitting in the hollow branch of an old willow tree, about 1.5 metres off the ground. The branch comes out almost horizontally (that is, nearly level) and has a hollow tunnel in it that goes more than a metre back.

The toad goes deep into the tunnel during the day and hides amongst the loose bits of rotten wood but at night comes further out and seems not to be bothered when I shine a torch beam on him. He sits quite still and the only movement is his pale, mottled throat gently moving in and out.

So I drew a picture of him.

Incidentally, I call him 'he' but I don't know whether it's a 'he' or a 'she'. It's hard to tell with toads unless they're in the water for breeding in the spring.

Apart from owls, there are several other flying creatures which come out at night. Some big beetles, especially cockchafers, blunder about on warm spring and summer nights, bumping into windows (or you); they're quite harmless.

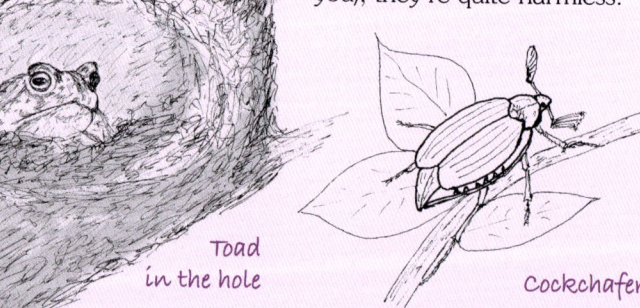

Toad in the hole

Cockchafer

Badger

Roe Deer

Garden Tiger Moth

Orange Red

Most moths are more active at night to find pale-coloured flowers with a good supply of nectar. Some species are also attracted by the scent of the flowers – some of which only smell strongly at night (e.g. night-scented stock, honeysuckle and tobacco plants).

Moths find each other by scent. They have a very good sense of smell – far better than ours, but then, most animals are better than us at sensing smells.

Moths are attracted to lights and will collect around lamps, even burning themselves by getting too close.

Isn't this odd for creatures that only come out in the dark?

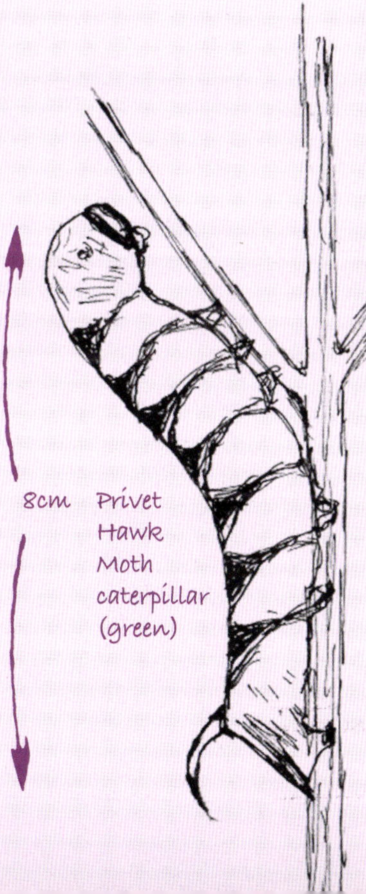

There are more than 40 times as many kinds of moth in the UK as there are butterflies and some of them are quite spectacular and some of their caterpillars are rather big.

8cm Privet Hawk Moth caterpillar (green)

However, the best place, by far, to look at in the dark is the pond. You can more or less be sure to see lots of interesting creatures. In fact, you can always see more by torchlight in a pond at night than you will ever see during the day. For example, one day in April in one of my ponds I could see only one smooth newt and a lot of water boatman.

When I revisited that night with my torch I counted 18 smooth newts, one very large (12cm in length) Great Crested Newt, two large diving beetles, lots of smaller beetles, several water lice and just as many pond snails and water boatmen as I saw in daylight.

The only creatures that I saw in daylight but not at night were pond skaters.

None of these animals were worried by the torchlight, even when shone closely on them, except the big diving beetles, which scuttled down to hide in the mud.

They are all more alarmed by any disturbance of the water.

Great Crested (or Warty) Newt

Just occasionally, you might be lucky and see a larger animal on the ground – most likely hedgehogs, foxes or rabbits – or in the bushes.

Mice do climb into bushes to collect berries or nuts and, again if you are especially lucky, you might see a dormouse.

If you do see a dormouse, normally this will be the Hazel Dormouse which eats hazel and other nuts, chestnuts and acorns, berries and fruits. It is about 7cm long and has a long bushy tail.

Dormouse

It hibernates from October to April so you will only see it in the summer – or, most likely, not at all. But it's still worth a look!

Useful words
that you may not have come across before

Abdomen – the hind section of insects and spiders. In rabbits (and us) it refers to what we usually call the stomach.

Algae – tiny plants, usually green or brown that turn water green and produce a thin green coating on the sides of ponds and on glass in greenhouses or fish tanks

Antennae – the 'feelers' on the heads of insects; used to touch things and detect scents

Aphids – also called greenfly or blackfly; small insects that suck the sap in plants

Camouflage – the appearance and colour of an animal that conceals itself from predators by attempting to appear like its surroundings, sometimes including dry bracken, dead leaves, bark etc.

Catkins – long, dangling flowers of many trees, sometimes short like the catkins on a pussy willow

Clutch – a group of eggs laid by a female bird

Cold-blooded – animals that simply have the same temperature as their surrounding

Digestion – what happens inside the stomach and intestines to convert food into juices that can be used by the body to build new tissue

Echo-location – sending out sound waves and receiving their echoes to find out where other objects are

Embryo – a developing animal (or plant)

Germination – the first stage in the development of seeds, when the first stem, leaf and roots emerge

Grub – another term for an insect larva, especially of bees, ants and beetles

Halteres – Little knobbed growths in place of the hind wings (for example in Daddy Long-legs)

Incubation – the process of keeping eggs warm so that the embryo develops and eventually hatches – as in birds and many reptiles like the grass snake

Larvae – the young of insects, such as caterpillars. One is called a 'larva'; the plural is 'larvae' (pronounced 'larvee').

Litter has two main meanings:
1. Young of dogs, cats, rabbits, mice etc.

2. Layer of dead leaves or sawdust used for bedding.

Mammals – animals that usually have fur, can regulate their body temperature (at 37°C) and suckle their young, providing warm milk for them to feed on and grow

Microbes – tiny creatures of many kinds, found everywhere. The soil is full of them but they are too small to see.

Mites – tiny creatures present in soil and many other places, with eight legs and rounded bodies

Moulting – shedding of the skin (in snakes) or coat (fur in cats, feathers in birds)

Nectar – sugary liquid produced by many flowers to attract insects, so that they spread pollen from one flower to another

Nocturnal – coming out only at night

Perch has two meanings:
1. The way a bird grips what it rests on
2. The place where this happens.

Pollen – tiny grains produced by plants that are needed to make seeds

Pollen baskets – shallow pits on a bumblebee's hind legs, used to carry pollen

Pollination – the act of carrying pollen from one flower to another

Predator – an animal that catches and eats another animal for food

Prey – animals eaten by other animals

Pupa – the hard case (usually brown) made by a caterpillar, inside which it changes into a butterfly or moth

Rhizomes – thick, underground stems that plants use to store food and spread out

Roost – a place where birds sleep

Runners – thin threads grown by plants, like strawberries, to spread out and grow new plants

Sap – the liquid inside plants, that moves water and food about, from roots to leaves, for example.

Security lights – lights on the outside of buildings that switch on when anyone (or an animal) comes near

Segment – small body section. Insects are divided into 3 segments and earthworms have many segments.

Surface tension – the way in which the surface of liquids holds onto small things that fall in

Tendrils – thin, green threads climbing plants use to hold on to supports

Vibrations – rapid shaking of ground when walked on, or water that is disturbed

Warm-blooded – animals that maintain the temperature of their bodies at a constant level

ACKNOWLEDGEMENTS AND PICTURE CREDITS
BY THE PUBLISHER

The author has produced all the black and white line drawings and the photos on p.17 (broken shells), p.29 (wasp nest), p.31 (yellow ant's hills) p.33 (magpie nest), p.34 (Mallard nest), p.33 (squirrel's drey, vole's nest), p.36 (rabbit burrow, badger sett), p.37 (grass snake), p.40 (Mallard ducklings), p.44 (red ants). Garden drawings on p.21 are by Robert Millard (top) and Lewis Elliott. The Professor Spedding character is by Tanya Warren. Photos on p.28 (catkins), p.29 (wasp), p.51 (acorns, conkers), p.52 (sunflower seeds), p.62 (banded snail), p.66 (detail of compound eye) are from iStock. The robin's nest photo on p.41 is by www.a-p-h-o-t-o.com. The photo on p.42 is © copyright Andy Potter and licensed for reuse under the Creative Commons License. All the butterfly photos are by Dr. Richard Harrington. The colour paintings are by the artist Isla Woiwod (http://www.woiwod.supanet.com).
Last but not least we most sincerely thank Dr. Kate Baker for kindly reviewing the manuscript and for her advice on the book's relevance to the national school curriculum.

We thank everyone for their wonderful contributions to this book.

OTHER NATURE BOOKS BY BRAMBLEBY BOOKS

Feathers and Eggshells
A bird journal of a young London girl
Natalie Lawrence
ISBN: 9780954334772 Hardback

Garden Photo Shoot
A Photographer's Year-book of Garden Wildlife
John Thurlbourn
ISBN 9780955392832 Paperback

Bird Words
Poetic images of wild birds
Hugh D. Loxdale
ISBN 9780954334734 Paperback

British and Irish Butterflies
Adrian Riley
ISBN 9780955392801 Paperback